RAY OF LIFE

E. L. TODD

RYKER

I walked Cheyenne to the door and gave her a kiss good night. I hadn't invited her to sleep over because I didn't want to share my bed with her. It was claustrophobic and uncomfortable. I didn't want to hold her all night and pretend to enjoy it. Truth was, I just wanted pussy.

She wrapped her arm around my neck as she kissed me aggressively, her small tongue darting into my mouth with eagerness. We'd just screwed and I made her come, but she wanted more.

I was satisfied.

She pulled away, but her body was still pressed hard into me. "You wanna get dinner tomorrow night?"

I didn't want to be an ass, but I wasn't interested in

seeing her again. It was better to be cold and honest than to leave her hanging. "I'm pretty busy. If you want to stop by sometime, give me call." That wasn't gentle either, but it was better than a simple no.

Her eyes fell when she understood what I meant. She should have expected this would happen eventually. I picked her up at a bar one night and took her back to my place. I'd never given her the impression I was looking for a woman to share my life with. I wanted something short with easy sex and decent conversation.

But now it was over.

"I'll see you around." She gave me another kiss before she walked away, her hair messy in the back from the way I gripped it earlier.

"Good night." I shut the door and walked back into my apartment. I was in my black sweatpants without a shirt, sexually satisfied but pathetically lonely. I stood in my living room and stared out the window to the bright skyscrapers of the city. I was on top of the world but at the bottom of my life.

Fuck, I missed Austen.

She and I were just hooking up, but the sex never felt meaningless. She and I were just hanging out, but it seemed like our friendship had lasted a lifetime. We were so artificial, but so deep at the same time.

I felt like I lost Rae all over again.

I fell back into my sofa and rested my neck on the

cushion. I stared up at the high ceiling, seeing the small art lights that dimly lit my apartment. It was quiet. I couldn't hear traffic from the street this high up. In Austen's apartment, the noise was obvious in any room because she was close to the bottom floor.

I missed that sound.

I pulled out my phone and checked for a message that I knew wouldn't exist. I wanted to ask Austen how her day was. I wanted to know if she went to the gym, even though I already knew the answer.

She said she hadn't gotten back together with Nathan, but I saw the way she kissed him. It was only a matter of time before they picked up where they left off. Months would go by, and then they would be living together, having the life they should have had years ago. I would just be a stepping stone, a name she would eventually forget.

Fuck, why hadn't I said something sooner?

Was I doomed to fuck up like this for the rest of my life?

Was I condemned to be alone forever?

I was lucky enough to meet two incredible women, but I lost both of them. Zeke was a good guy and a worthy opponent. But Nathan didn't deserve Austen. He should have kept his dick in his pants when he had a woman like that waiting at home for him.

I was disappointed in her. I understood she loved the

guy. I even believed he would get it right this time. But that didn't erase the past. It didn't change the mistake he made. Maybe Austen could forget about it, but I never would.

I sat on that couch for a long time, listening to the distant hum of my refrigerator as it made ice. I could have turned on the TV just to have something to look at, but I didn't. I absorbed my isolation like a sponge, feeling on top of the world but so low at the same time. I had so much to be grateful for, but I was utterly miserable.

I looked at my phone again and wrote a message to Austen.

I fucking miss you. My depression was doing all the talking in that moment. My heart was on my sleeve, and I didn't care how aggressive I was being. But then reality clicked in, and I erased the words in the box and tossed my phone aside.

I couldn't be trusted with that thing.

At least not tonight.

My week was uneventful. I hit the gym every day, but played video games for the rest of the time. The guys asked me to go out, but I chose to stay home and wallow in my solitude. When I focused on a task, like a video game, it usually distracted me enough so I wouldn't think about the woman I lost.

Did I ever really have her?

She wanted to be with a cheating asshole over me.

What a fucking insult.

Liam had been right the whole time. He warned me Austen would break my heart, and I was too arrogant to think I could be a victim. But that woman got me good. My heart had already been broken, but she managed to break it all over again.

Now I was even more convinced of my feelings for her. I continued to shrug them off for so long, living in denial. But the truth was right in front of me the entire time. I was still hung up on Rae, but Austen was definitely taking her place.

I hadn't spoken to Austen in a week, and I was beginning to lose my mind. I just wanted a conversation with her, something normal. I took our closeness for granted, our wonderful friendship. I could tell her anything without fear of judgment. I couldn't say that about very many people.

My phone rang, and Liam's name popped up on the screen. I didn't want to talk to anyone, but when Liam was involved, there was always a possibility Austen wouldn't be too far behind. I answered. "What's up, man?"

"I haven't talked to you all week. What's new with you?"

Just thriving in despair. "I've been working on stuff for my family's company. You know, paperwork and what not."

"Sounds like a snooze fest."

"You could say that." I held the phone between my shoulder and neck and kept playing with the game on mute. He could probably hear my fingers tapping against the buttons of my controller.

"You wanna go out tonight? Madeline wants to try this new vegan place. I'm not thrilled about it, but you know, I want pussy, so whatever."

I chuckled into the phone. "No, you don't. Stop trying to be macho."

"What are you talking about? Of course I do."

"Madeline isn't pussy, and you know it. You like this woman. Just own up to it."

Liam sighed into the phone. "Fine, I like her. You wanna come?"

"As the third wheel?"

"No, I think Austen and Jenn are going to be there." He paused to wait for my reaction. "Unless, you don't really want to be around Austen anymore."

It was in my best interest to stay away from her, to protect what remained of my broken heart. But damn, I missed her like crazy. I wanted to see her, to laugh with her. "You know I don't have a problem with her."

"Well, you seemed pretty—"

"I'm fine, Liam." I wasn't going to admit my heartbreak to another person. I didn't want Liam to rub his advice in my face. "Just let me know what time, and I'll be there."

———

I can't remember the last time I was this nervous.

Acid had built up in my stomach, and I felt nauseated. A part of me couldn't wait to be with Austen again, to hug her again. But another part of me wanted to get the hell out of there and spare me the pain.

Liam and I got there first, and a moment later, Austen and Madeline walked inside. Jenn was nowhere to be found.

Austen wore a strapless yellow sundress with a gold necklace around her throat. Her dark hair was in loose curls that trailed down her shoulders. She was stunning —like always.

I was rock-hard.

I gawked at her as she walked inside, those long legs extended underneath her dress. She wore nude heels. I liked it when she wore heels. It was easier for me to bend down and kiss her. I was mesmerized by her appearance, her sheer elegance.

Wow, I missed her.

I rose to my feet because my legs were thinking on their own. Liam did the same when he realized his date was there. He turned and embraced her, leaving Austen and me alone to look at each other.

We just stared.

It was tense.

Awkward.

Strange.

I couldn't take my eyes off her. She was gorgeous from head to toe, and those pretty eyes did strange things to my gut. My lips ached for hers, and I longed for those nights we used to share together. "Hey, Stone Cold." I forced the words out of my mouth and the smile that followed afterward.

She immediately smiled at the nickname, an automatic response. "Hey."

I moved in to hug her because it felt strange not greeting her in an ordinary fashion. I wrapped my arms around her and allowed them to rest on her hips. It gave me the opportunity to hide my face and smell her hair.

She smelled amazing.

She hugged me back, letting the embrace linger just the way I did.

Would it be totally inappropriate if I kissed her?

Friends kiss, right?

Austen pulled away just in time. She was testing my patience by looking so beautiful. It was absolute torture. "How are you?"

Terrible.

Depressed.

Lost.

"Good. You?"

"Yeah…good."

We sat down, and the waiter took our drink orders. Austen sat across from me so it felt like we were on a double date.

A date would be nice.

"Jared broke up with that girl he was seeing," Madeline said.

"He did?" Liam blurted. "Why? She was hot."

Austen kicked him under the table at the exact same time I did.

Austen and I exchanged a quick look, feeling our legs touch together. Just that got me hot. I missed the way those beautiful legs used to wrap around my waist while I fucked her hard into the mattress.

Calm down, Ryker.

Madeline didn't seem upset by Liam's stupid comment. "I don't know. He didn't tell me why."

"That's a shame," Austen said. "I liked her. She was a good bowler too."

Austen told me that Jared had a thing for Madeline. I wondered if that had anything to do with their breakup. Maybe Liam had competition on the horizon. He should seal the deal now while he had the chance. You never know when another guy will come along and steal your woman.

I know from experience.

We ordered our lunch then handed over the menus. I just picked something at random because I wasn't a vegan kind of guy. I need some serious protein in my diet, mainly chicken and fish. I couldn't eat greens all day like Madeline. Liam was in for a tough road.

Since Austen was sitting directly across from me, I had nothing else to do besides stare at her. It was easy to do and enjoyable. I remembered the way those soft strands felt between my fingertips. I remembered the way those soft lips felt against mine.

I remembered everything.

Did she?

I wanted to ask about Nathan, but I didn't want to know the answer. She said she wasn't seeing him, but after that kiss, I suspected it was bound to happen. I couldn't compete with the man she was going to marry.

Luck wasn't on my side.

"Did you catch the Met game the other night?" Austen finally asked, breaking the stare down we had against each other.

It took a moment for me to absorb her words and understand what she was saying. I kept picturing her underneath me on the bed, taking a pounding that made her come. "Yeah, I did." I stared at the screen without really watching it. I caught the score here and there. But if anything significant happened, I missed it. "You?"

"Yeah."

Did she watch it with Nathan? I missed being able to talk to her how I wanted, to be honest. Now I was walking on eggshells, steering away from topics neither one of us wanted to broach.

It sucked.

She didn't ask me about Cheyenne. I wanted to tell her I wasn't seeing her anymore, but that wouldn't make any difference. I would just pick up someone new in a few days…and then someone new after that. The cycle would continue indefinitely.

And so would my misery.

We all said goodbye on the sidewalk and went our separate ways. Austen and I happened to live in the same direction, so we walked side by side. My hands were in my pockets because I didn't trust them. They wanted to grab those womanly hips and force her into my chest. "What are you up to now?"

"Just heading home. What about you?"

I didn't want to go home. I'd been inside all week, with the exception of my gym visits. "I'll probably watch the Yankees." I didn't have anything else to do, and watching sports was a great way to stop my depressing thoughts.

"Yeah, me too."

My brain flipped on me and the words flew out of my mouth. "You wanna watch it with me?" I didn't know what the hell I was doing, but the damage was done. The question was out in the universe and could never be taken back.

"Sure."

Really? I wanted to jump in the air and even do a little dance like a moron. "Cool. Let's pick up some beers on the way." I stopped by a convenience store and picked up a six-pack before we entered my building. We took the elevator to the top before we entered my lonely apartment. I popped off two caps and handed her a bottle.

She took a look around like she expected the place to look different since the last time she visited. She took a seat on one side of the couch, purposely keeping her distance.

I was disappointed, but I wasn't sure what I was expecting in the first place. I sat in my usual spot and turned on the game.

She crossed her legs and drank her beer. When she wasn't drinking, she played with the top of the bottle by sliding her fingers around the glass. Even something as boring as her fingers were sexy.

I was so excited to get her here, but now that she was right beside me, I didn't know what to do. It didn't feel the same way it used to. She wasn't ten feet away—but it felt like ten miles. "How's work?" It was such a simple question, but my arsenal was empty at the moment.

"About the same. I got a new treadmill desk."

"Cool. Sounds dangerous though."

"It's fine when I'm typing emails and making phone calls."

"I'm surprised you have the coordination for that," I teased.

She smirked then tossed a throw pillow at me.

I placed it under my arm so I would be even more comfortable. "Thanks."

"Asshole," she said with a repressed grin.

I focused on the game again, doing my best not to look at her. Despite our distance, this was the best I'd felt all week. Just having her nearby eased my pain. There was something about her presence that I found innately soothing. "So, how are things with Nathan?" I didn't know why I just sabotaged my small amount of happiness with the idiotic question. I didn't want to listen to her tell me she was still in love with the guy.

E. L. TODD

"They aren't going," she said. "I told you I'm not seeing him."

I wanted to believe her—more than anything in the world. "Then what was that kiss about? Why were you guys drinking together and watching the game?" I did my best to keep the accusation out of my tone, but it was a struggle. I couldn't get mad at her for spending time with other men, but I certainly didn't appreciate being lied to.

"His friend lives in my building, so he stopped by and asked if I wanted to get a drink."

And why the fuck did she say yes? "Why did you go with him?"

She shrugged, her eyes on the TV. "I don't know…I just did."

Not a good enough reason for me.

"We were watching the game, and then he leaned in… It happened so fast."

"You kissed him for fifteen seconds, so it wasn't that fast." I knew exactly how long it lasted because I caught most of it from the front row. It definitely wasn't a kiss she didn't want. I could read it all over her face.

She finally turned to me, annoyance in her eyes. "Excuse me?"

"I just don't appreciate being lied to. He kissed you, and you kissed him back. Don't turn it around and make it seem like you didn't want it."

"I never said that." Her voice rose, along with her anger.

"Sounded like it."

She set down her beer like she was about to storm off. "Why are you being an asshole right now?"

"I'm not. I'm just not a big fan of lying. After everything you've been through, I thought you would feel the same way."

I hit a nerve. I could see it written across that once beautiful face. Now she looked pissed. If she had a knife, it would be in my neck right now. "Wow...that was low."

I felt like shit the moment I said it. I wished I could take it back.

She got off the couch, making her dramatic exit. Her heels tapped against the hardwood floor as she headed out of there.

I fucked up. I had to make it right. "Austen, wait."

"Fuck you, Ryker." She grabbed her purse off the counter and bolted to the door.

"Hold on." I hopped over the couch and shut the door just as she opened it. "I'm sorry, alright? It was a dumbass thing to say."

She yanked on the door handle, but the door didn't move, not with my weight pressed against it. "Then why the hell did you say it? You were nice a second ago, and then you turned into a huge bitch face."

I didn't appreciate the insult, but I let it go. "I don't

know why I said it…" That wasn't the whole truth, definitely an exaggerated lie.

She crossed her arms over her chest, her eyes narrowing in hostility.

Even when she did that, I thought she was cute. "Okay…I do know why I said it."

She shifted her weight to one hip as she waited.

For better or for worse, I was gonna tell her the truth. Maybe it would just push her further away. Maybe it wouldn't. I was about to find out. "When I saw you kiss him—"

"He kissed me."

"Whatever." It didn't matter to me. Their lips were locked, and that was enough to make me sick. "I felt like shit. I haven't been knocked out like that since…Rae picked Zeke over me." I remembered that night vividly, and it was frightening how similar they were. "I'm not gonna sugarcoat it. It fucking hurt, Austen."

Her attitude dropped instantly, and her features softened like my words actually meant something to her.

"You didn't tell me you were seeing him again. It was so sudden."

"I wasn't seeing him."

"But you were spending time with him. I thought we told each other everything? Why didn't you mention that to me?"

Now she looked guilty. "I don't know… I didn't see any reason to mention it. It didn't mean anything to me. And I knew how you felt about him, so I didn't want to bring it up."

I pressed my back against the door even though she wasn't trying to get out anymore. "I guess I'm not handling this Nathan thing very well. You tell me you aren't seeing him anymore, but you're kissing him in bars…"

"It wasn't like that."

"I shouldn't care. You're free to do whatever you want. But it hurt. I got jealous…really jealous."

She stepped closer to me, her hand moving to my arm. "Well…I wasn't happy about your date either. I was pretty upset, actually."

"You were?" I whispered.

"Of course." She stared down at the ground, her long eyelashes beautiful and thick. "I was really jealous. I felt terrible, like someone stepped on my neck so I couldn't breathe."

"Yeah?" That confession shouldn't have made me happy, but it did.

"Yeah."

My fingers moved under her chin, and I lifted her gaze. "Let's be honest with each other. Right here, right now."

She held my gaze, her eyes shifting back and forth to look at mine since she was standing so close to me.

"Do you still love Nathan?"

She closed her eyes for several seconds, thinking about her answer before she gave it. "Yes. Do you still love Rae?"

That woman was still on my mind. I found myself wondering what she was doing, if she was thinking about me at the same time I was thinking about her. I wanted to move on and forget her for good, but I couldn't. "Yes." I answered her question, so now it was my turn to ask something. "Do you want to get back together with Nathan?"

She closed her eyes again as she considered the question. "Sometimes. But when I kissed him in that bar, I thought about you. That was why I ended it…because I realized I wanted to be with you more."

It was a confession I didn't expect to hear. "You want to be with me?"

"Yes and no."

"Why not?"

"Because she's still on your mind…just how Nathan is still on my mind. These people broke both of us. I'm not sure if we could ever make it work, not when we have this kind of baggage. And then you hooked up with that woman…"

Now I wished I hadn't. "So, where does that leave us?"

"I don't know…"

In the three months that I spent with Austen, I knew she made me happy. When I was with her, I didn't think about Rae. But I didn't have much to offer her. I was damaged goods. If I couldn't put myself back together, could I put her back together?

"If Rae wanted to be with you again, would you do it?" she asked. "If she realized she made a mistake and left her boyfriend?"

That was a difficult question because it would never happen. Rae made up her mind and she wasn't going to change it. She stuck to her guns. "That would never happen."

"But if it did."

"If it did…" If Rae really showed up on my doorstep and wanted to spend her life with me, I'd have a hard time turning her down. "I would take her back." Even though that would end my relationship with Austen, I knew who I would choose.

Austen nodded like she'd been expecting that answer. "I'm so confused about Nathan. I've been so heartbroken for years because I thought he was the one. I still love him and want to be with him, and I just can't let go of the past. But I wish I could. I wish I could have the life we didn't get the chance to have."

If Rae cheated on me, I'd take her back too. I knew I would. When you fell in love, you never really fell out of it. "If that's how you really feel, you should give him another chance." I couldn't believe I was saying this, but I felt compelled to. Austen was my closest friend. I wanted the best for her even if that made me miserable in the process. "Because if he's your Rae, you shouldn't let him go."

"Really?" she whispered. "You really think that?"

I nodded.

"But I want to be with you." She moved farther into my chest, resting her face against my pec.

My arms circled her waist. "I want to be with you too. But I can't offer you what he can. I don't know if I'll ever be over Rae. I don't know if I'll ever be in a place to have a life with someone. I can't give you what you deserve."

She wrapped her arms around my neck and looked up into my face. "Ever?"

I shrugged. "Maybe."

"So…can we still be friends?" she whispered. "Because this past week has been torture without you."

"It's been torture for me too. Yes, I want to still see you. I still want to get a beer with you and watch the game. I still want to split a plate of fries with you."

"I do too." When she looked up at me, her lips were

slightly parted and her eyelids were heavy. She rose gently on her tiptoes so she could be closer to my lips.

I tugged her closer to my chest and pressed my lips to hers. My lips immediately moved with her plump mouth, and my tongue dived into her mouth. It'd been a week since I had her, a week of torture. Now that we were reunited again, I didn't want to let her go.

I guided her to my bedroom down the hall without breaking our kiss. Our mouths moved harder together as clothes started to come off. Cheyenne was an easy lay so I was physically satisfied, but I was never emotionally happy. With Austen, all my fantasies and desires were fulfilled—a million times over.

I got her on the foot of the bed and kicked my bottoms off. My cock was throbbing in desperate need to be inside her. I only fucked Cheyenne with a condom, so I knew I could go bareback with Austen.

I never wanted to fuck her with a rubber.

I moved my hands behind her knees and dragged her ass to the edge of the bed. My cock twitched in anticipation because I missed her all week. This may be the last time I got to be with her, and I was going to make it count.

I pressed my thumb to her clitoris and rubbed her aggressively as I slipped two fingers inside her pussy. She was warm and wet like I expected. I'd never explored her in disappointment. I leaned over her and pressed my mouth against hers as I continued to work her clit, making her writhe underneath me in preparation for my hard cock. Our tongues danced together, and I breathed deeply into her mouth, my spine tensing in preparation for this beautiful woman.

When I couldn't wait any longer, I pulled my fingers out and stroked them along my length, lubing the head of my hard dick. My sticky fingers wrapped around the base and I pushed inside her entrance, sliding through that tight cunt I'd come to worship. I slid through her slickness until I was completely sheathed.

I took a moment to enjoy her, pausing to concentrate on this unbelievably tight pussy. My arms locked behind her knees, and I leaned over to get a good look at her beautiful face. Her hands moved up my chest, her nails gently dragging into my skin as she moved. Her lips were parted like she wanted more of my tongue.

Could I really walk away from this?

She dragged her hands down my back then gripped my ass. She pulled me out then tugged me back in. "Fuck me, Ryker."

Jesus Christ.

"Yes, sweetheart." That was one of the most erotic moments of my life. I pounded into her pussy just the way she ordered—good and hard. Her slickness increased and her pussy tightened around my big cock the way it always did.

Her hands moved to my chest then my arms, and soon her chest was sleek with sweat. It gleamed under the light from the ceiling and made her tits look gorgeous. Moans escaped her lips, that perfect mouth open and her white teeth showing.

I stared at her tongue as I thrust into her, loving every little feature about her. I could fuck her like this every day for the rest of my life. "Sweetheart…" My body and mind combined into one entity, and my senses were heightened. All I felt were the primal sensations from my gut, the need to screw this woman and never stop. I'd never been so focused on one woman before. With the precision of a surgeon, I took her with purpose, hitting her in the right spot every time. I gripped her tit then kissed her, my tongue dancing with hers.

"Ryker…" She said my name in the sexiest way, sounding like an angel but a naughty girl at the exact same time. "I'm already gonna come."

"Good. I'll make you come again."

Her nails dug into me in response, and she gasped through the sensation that rocked her body. Her head rolled back and her eyes landed on the ceiling. Her screams turned into incoherent moans, a jumble of emotions that hit her at the exact same time.

I felt like a king.

And I wished she were my queen.

2

AUSTEN

I didn't want to leave.

I woke up before he did, before my alarm clock pierced the bedroom with its shrillness. His arms were wrapped around me and his chest was pressed against my back. He was just as sexy when he was asleep as when he was awake. His jaw wasn't as hard as it usually was, and his beard was thicker than it was when we went to sleep the night before. His hair was all over the place because I dug my fingers through it so many times.

He was perfect.

I knew when I walked out of that apartment, I would never return as a fuck buddy or love interest. He told me he had feelings for me, something more meaningful than carnal sex, but that wasn't enough for either one of us. He was still into Rae, and I was still into Nathan.

Our timing was terrible.

He said he could never give me what I deserved, and I didn't want to settle for half of his heart. He didn't deserve half of mine either.

Just being friends was the best option for both of us.

But I knew I would miss him like crazy.

My alarm went off and shredded the silence.

I snatched the phone and immediately turned it off, but the unsettling way it erupted in our ears couldn't be shaken. Ryker stirred from his position, his arms tightening around me and a sigh escaping his throat. "Why do you wake up so damn early?"

"Because I have to work—unlike some people."

"Then stop working."

"I need money for food, rent, and clothes."

"All those things are overrated." He pulled me tighter against his body, his strong arms caging me in like steel. "You can live here for free. Eat my food. And we both know you don't need clothes."

"I sound like a pet."

"A very cute pet." He kissed my neck and smelled my hair.

It would be impossible for me to leave now, not with this strong and sexy man asking me to stay with him. It seemed like we both wanted to forget the conversation we had the night before. I was almost tempted to change my mind about everything. "I should get going..." I didn't want to leave after our incredible night, but I knew I had to. I'd be late for the third time this month if I didn't get my ass in gear.

Ryker reluctantly let me go and pulled on his sweatpants.

After I got dressed, we met at the front door.

Ryker ran his fingers through his messy hair and blinked his sleepy eyes. He stared at the door then released a heavy sigh, like he was dreading the next part of our morning.

I was dreading it too. "I don't like this either..."

"I'm glad I'm not the only one." He leaned against the door and placed his hands in his pockets. His abs were tight all the way down to his hips, where the large V disappeared into his pants. I loved the veins just above his cock. He was so corded and lean. I loved that beautiful body on top of mine when it was all sweaty and delicious.

I needed to get my head out of the gutter. We could repeat everything we said the night before, but that wouldn't make things easier. "I guess I'll see you around..."

"Yeah. There's a game on Friday. Wanna watch it?"

At least I had something to look forward to. It made this goodbye a little less painful. "Sure." I moved for the door, not expecting a goodbye kiss that could make this more difficult.

Ryker grabbed me by the door and yanked me toward him. "You're still mine for the next thirty seconds." He pressed his mouth to mine and kissed me, his tongue immediately greeting mine despite the fact neither one of us had brushed our teeth. His arms pulled me tight against him, making me feel like the only woman in the world.

My arms circled his waist, and I clung to him desperately, missing him before I even left.

His hand dug into my hair, and he sucked my bottom lip into his mouth. He breathed with me, those breaths filling my lungs. He breathed life back into me, making me feel something I hadn't felt in years. I spent all my time trying to feel nothing, and he was the first man to make me feel something again.

He reluctantly pulled away, the sadness obvious in his blue eyes. "Have a good day at work." His mouth uttered those words, but his eyes said something else entirely. They told me all the things he couldn't say, all the painful words I didn't want to hear.

"Yeah…have a good day playing Call of Duty."

He forced a chuckle. "I will."

I got the door open and walked out, not wasting any time by lingering. The situation was like a bandage. The sooner I got it off, the sooner all of this would be over. I could forget the pain and move on. It wasn't like I loved the guy. "See you later."

He held on to the door and nodded. "See you later."

When I walked away, I didn't look back. I didn't want to see the sadness on his face. I may not love him, but he was certainly in my heart. He'd become my closest friend, the person I confided everything to. But he wasn't mine to keep, and I was too broken to be put back together.

So I kept going.

I was just as sad that week as I was the previous week.

I stayed home most of the time and ate everything in my fridge. I was too bummed to head to the store, so I ordered a lot of delivery, mainly greasy Chinese food because there was a place just a block from me. I could get off my ass and get it myself, but even that was too much work for someone with no motivation.

Friday couldn't come soon enough. I kept wanting to tell Ryker about my life throughout the week, but I realized that wouldn't be right. Platonic friends didn't do that, unless they were girls like Madeline, Jenn, and I. And even then, we only shared the important stuff. Madeline wouldn't care about my piece of orange chicken that kinda looked like the state of Texas. Ryker would, but I still couldn't interrupt his life to tell him about it.

Had he already been with another woman by now?

Probably.

That chased away my appetite.

My phone vibrated on the coffee table, and I immediately snatched it, hoping to see Ryker's name on the screen.

It was Nathan. *I'm about to go for a jog. Wanna come?*

Exercise was the very last thing I wanted to do. I could barely get up when I had to pee. I usually held it as long as possible until my bladder couldn't take anymore. It wasn't healthy, but that's how down I was. *No thanks. Not in the mood.*

What are you in the mood for?

Chinese food and ice cream. Nathan was a bit of a health freak, so he never had the same cravings. Ryker was the same way. He usually had chicken and vegetables for dinner, the most boring meal on the planet.

Then let's get Chinese food and ice cream.

You hate that stuff.

I don't hate it when I'm with you.

The only reason I didn't roll my eyes was because he was being sincere. *I'm no fun right now. Maybe next week.*

Now I really want to see you. I'll meet you at Golden Dragon in fifteen minutes. Better not stand me up.

I'm not kidding. I'm terrible company right now.

And it sounds like you need a friend. I want to be that friend.

We sat in one of the rundown booths in the corner and ate our combination plates. I had chow mein and rice, along with kung pao chicken. When we first walked in, the delivery guy talked to me like I was a regular.

That was a little embarrassing.

Nathan didn't bombard me with questions right away. He ate and asked me about work and if I liked my dinner. He wore a slimming dark blue t-shirt, making his shoulders and chest look nice.

I'd never been into two guys at the same time, and I felt a little slutty because of it. I missed Ryker and thought he was the sexiest guy on the planet, and then when I was with Nathan, I thought the exact same thing about him.

I didn't know that was possible.

"What's on your mind?" he finally asked. His grilled vegetables and chow mein were pushed to the side. He didn't eat most of it, probably because it was greasy and fattening.

I was grateful I was a woman. Ryker liked my curves, my round ass and belly. I wouldn't have the discipline to eat clean and work out all the time if I were a man. I'd let myself get soft and wouldn't think twice about it. "Ryker and I stopped seeing each other…"

"Oh…" He nodded slowly, his jaw suddenly becoming tense.

I knew this would make Nathan uncomfortable, but I'd rather be transparent than mysterious. "We agreed that we seriously liked each other, but it would never work out. He's still into his ex, and I'm still into you…" I didn't feel uncomfortable because Nathan already knew how I felt. In fact, he knew I was still in love with him. "So we decided it was best to just stay friends. Our hearts aren't in the right place. But, I'm pretty bummed out about it."

"Sounds like you really liked him."

"I did…I do." Ryker was a great guy—one of a kind. "But he says he can never give me what I deserve, something serious. And I don't want to be with him when I'm not over you. Not fair to him…not fair to me."

"Makes sense." He massaged his knuckles on the table, a habit he used to do when he was anxious. "Does that mean you're going to give me a chance?"

I hadn't mentioned that part just yet. I didn't want to come out and say it. For some reason, I found it difficult. "I'm open to the idea." It would be stupid to lay out all my cards on the table for him to see.

His mouth slowly rose into a smile. "That's great…

really." He swallowed hard when he lost his voice. "I won't mess this up again. Promise."

I couldn't believe I was sitting across from him after he cheated on me. He betrayed my trust and broke my heart. I'd never been the same since that horrible day I walked in on him with Lily. But now I was sitting across from him, butterflies still in my stomach. Any sane person would say this was a mistake, and he didn't deserve a second chance. But my heart disagreed. "I'm ready for some ice cream. Are you?"

He still wore that giant grin, the happiness reaching his eyes. "Absolutely."

I was waiting for Ryker to walk inside the bar, my stomach all tied up in knots, when Jared walked in.

"Hey, stranger." He gave me a one-arm hug before he sat on the stool beside me. "What brings you here?"

I held up my bottle. "The beer and fries."

"Ah, should have known." He waved down the bartender and ordered a beer before he turned back to me. "Trying to pick up another boy toy? I thought you already had two men snagged on your line?"

"Now I have none, unfortunately."

"What happened with Ryker? You seemed to be into him."

I talked to Jared just the way I talked to Madeline, all my girly feelings out in the open. "He's in love with some woman... I'm still in love with Nathan. It just didn't work out. But we're good friends."

"That's a shame," he said. "He's a cool guy."

"He is a cool guy."

"You know I'm not a fan of Nathan." Jared covered his brooding look with a drink from his beer.

"You wouldn't be the only one." None of the girls liked him either. Nathan would really have to bust his ass to change their minds. "I'm not even sure if Nathan is gonna be around. We're just...taking it slow. We hang out here and there, but there's nothing physical going on."

"For now," he said. "He'll make his move shortly. I just hope you know what you're doing. Once a cheater, always a cheater."

"I don't think that's totally true. We all make mistakes."

"Well, that was a pretty big mistake," he snapped. "You guys were gonna get married, as in, spend the rest of your lives together. And then he pulled that shit. I love you, Austen, but you're better than this. Don't you want your husband to be the guy you trust above anyone else?"

Ryker's face came into my mind. He was honest to a fault.

"I didn't say I was gonna marry the guy. Again, we're taking things slow."

"You know, if you really put yourself back on the market, you could get a pretty incredible guy. You don't have to give Nathan another chance."

I knew Jared would give me his two cents until I shut him up. "I get that, Jared. But the way I feel about Nathan is the way you feel about Madeline."

The instant I called him out on his true feelings, he fell silent.

"I can't help it," I said quietly. "I wish I could just forget about him and move on with my life. But in the past three years, I haven't been successful—at all. I still think about him, dream about him. And Ryker said if I feel this strongly about him, I should try to make it work. Because love like that doesn't happen very often."

"I guess he's talking from experience?"

I nodded.

"I'm sorry I was so harsh before. I just love you, Austen. I want you to be with a guy who only makes you smile, you know? I meant well."

I rubbed his arm. "I know you did."

"I didn't realize I was being so obvious about Maddie…"

I nodded.

"Does she know?"

"No."

He took a longer drink of his beer this time, nearly finishing it off. "Your brother is a nice guy, but I really hate him."

I chuckled. "I've heard that before."

"I should have done something sooner. But now it's too late."

This conversation was a conflict of interest since Liam was my brother. It was obvious how much he liked Maddie. But Jared was one of my best friends, and I wanted him to be happy. "I don't know what to say. I would tell you to go for her, but she does seem pretty into Liam."

"That's what I feared." He finished his beer then waved down the bartender for another even though we'd only been sitting there for ten minutes.

"Sorry, Jared."

He clinked his beer against mine. "I'm sorry too. All those happy endings people told us about when we were kids were bullshit. You don't just fall in love with someone and that's the end of the story. Love stinks."

"Yeah, it does."

Jared and I fell into comfortable silence as we watched the game, each of us drowning in the beer that was shoved down our throats.

"Hope you saved me some." Ryker appeared on the other side of me, looking handsome in a black t-shirt.

His eyes smiled when he looked at me, like he'd missed me all week.

"I couldn't drink everything in this bar if I tried."

"But you could eat all the fries, that's for sure." He gave me a gentle poke in the side before he waved down the bartender. It was a pretty blonde now, and she didn't waste any time getting him what he needed. "The lady and I will split an order of garlic fries too."

Her smile fell once she assumed Ryker was with me. "Coming right up."

Ryker waved to Jared. "Hey, man. You came out to watch the game."

"Ran into Austen by coincidence," Jared said. "I'm just lucky like that."

The three of us enjoyed the game as friends, accepting the comfortable silence as our eyes were glued to the TV. Only when commercials were on did we make conversation, and we mostly stuck to the topic of sports.

At the end of the game when the score was determined, Ryker mentioned Nathan. "So, have you guys been hanging out?"

I didn't know why he tortured himself with the question. I didn't want to know about the bimbos he'd picked up during the week. "We went out for Chinese food the other day. Then we got some ice cream. But that was about it." I didn't want Ryker to think I slept with Nathan when I didn't.

He tossed another fry into his mouth, probably so he would have something to do instead of just staring at me. "Is it going somewhere?"

"I don't know. We're just taking it slow right now."

Ryker ate another fry, his eyes downcast. "Excuse me." He walked around the corner and into the bathroom.

Jared turned in his stool until he faced me. "He's so into you. It's obvious."

"I'm into him too."

"Wouldn't you rather make it work with an honest guy like him than a cheater?"

Absolutely. "But Ryker is in love with someone else. I told you that."

"And you're in love with Nathan. It's perfect."

"Perfect how?" It was anything but perfect. Our feelings for each other were mostly lustful and artificial. That wasn't how love was supposed to be.

"Get over your exes together."

3

RYKER

My phone rang and my brother's name appeared on the screen. "Hey, is COLLECT still standing?"

"For the most part," he said with a chuckle. "But I need some help, actually."

"Me doing all the paperwork isn't enough help?" I was still handling almost everything from home. I took care of the consultants, the legal team, and all the other stuff that kept the company running.

"It is," he said. "But I was hoping you could come down and cover for me for a week."

"Cover for you?" I wasn't going back to Seattle. No way. I already did that once and got my heart stomped on. That shit didn't feel good. "You can't go on a vacation right now. You've only been there for six months."

"It's not a vacation. Believe me, I wish it were."

Now that my father had died of cancer, I took health more seriously. When someone was down, that's what my thoughts immediately jumped to. "Everything alright, man?"

"I'm having surgery in a few days. Getting my gall bladder removed. Nothing serious."

I leaned back into the sofa and let the relief seep out of my pores. "Scared me for a second."

"Nothing to be worried about. The doctor said I could go back to work two days after the surgery, but I'm gonna take it easy for the rest of the week. I'm sorry to drag you back here when you just left not too long ago, but I don't trust anyone else to cover for me."

"It's no problem," I said quickly. "I'm happy to do it." If my family needed me for anything, I was there. If he really was just taking a trip to Hawaii, that was a different story. But surgery was a perfectly acceptable excuse.

"Thanks, man. Mom will be excited."

She'd be over the moon to see me again so soon. She still called me all the time. "Yeah, I know."

"Alright, talk to you later."

"See ya."

I hung up and tossed the phone on the couch. Now I

had to return to the same city where Rae was living her happy life with that asshole Zeke. Okay, he wasn't an asshole. Pretty stand-up guy, actually. But I would always be jealous of him. He had Rae in his bed every night while I had absolutely nothing here in New York.

Well, I had Austen.

Actually, I *used* to have Austen.

Now I was alone.

I considered telling Rae that I was stopping by. It'd be nice to see her again, to get dinner or something, but that was a disaster waiting to happen. I couldn't sit across from her and not think about kissing her, fucking her, and doing all the things I used to do. It would put stress on her relationship with Zeke, which isn't something I wanted to happen. I'd be lying if I said I didn't have fantasies about Rae and Zeke breaking up. Rae would come back to me and want to start over. But I always pushed those thoughts away because Rae would be heartbroken if she lost Zeke.

I didn't want her to be miserable.

It was unlikely Rae and I would run into each other at work or anywhere else, so I was going to keep my visit a secret. If I stayed in my office, no one would know about it anyway. So everything would work out just fine.

I hadn't hooked up with anyone since Austen and I broke things off. I'd thought about it a few times, but after fooling around with Cheyenne, I realized it was a waste of time. Hooking up with strangers didn't feel good anymore. It was meaningless and downright sad. The woman kept looking at me like I might be her future husband, and I could hardly remember her name.

It was best to be alone.

Maybe when enough time passed, I could meet a nice woman and start over. It was unlikely, but I could dream, right?

When I pictured myself with someone long term, Austen's face came to mind. Even when we weren't screwing, we had a great time together. I could watch a game with her and devour a pack of beers at the same time. I couldn't say that about many women —except Rae.

But Austen wanted to be with Nathan.

I accepted that. When Rae wanted to be with Zeke, I let her go. And now I would let Austen go too.

Why the fuck did I have to be such a nice guy?

I lay in bed with the lights off and looked out the window. The skyscrapers were bright against the night sky in the background, and distant blinking lights from planes and helicopters could be seen as they moved past my window.

I couldn't sleep, so I just watched the pretty lights,

my sheets smelling like nothing since I just washed them. Loose strands of Austen's hair were nowhere in sight. I couldn't smell her scent anymore either.

It was like she was never there at all.

The thought of Austen made me horny. It was impossible not to get aroused when I thought about her beautiful hair and perfect lips. I'd have to be a robot not to get hard when I thought about that gorgeous woman.

But my desire was mixed with sadness.

I missed her. Not her pussy, her ass, and her tits.

Just her.

Like she knew I was thinking about her, she called. The phone lit up and vibrated on the nightstand with her name on the screen. My dick was hard under the sheets, but I didn't feel guilty about it.

I took the call. "Hey, sweetheart." The nickname slipped out because I wasn't thinking. But since she was calling me at nearly midnight, I figured this wasn't a friendly phone call. Maybe she wanted some action. And if that's what she wanted, I wasn't going to say no.

I'm only human.

"Hey." That soft voice came through the phone, melodic and comforting. She could be an actress if she wanted to. With those beautiful looks and that sexy voice, she would be unstoppable. "Am I calling too late?"

"Never."

"You don't have a guest over?"

I found the question insulting when I shouldn't. "Just me in this big bed…all alone."

"My bed is small, so I don't feel quite as alone."

I assumed Nathan wasn't there, but I was glad she'd confirmed it. "How was your week?" I hadn't spoken to her since last Friday when we watched the game together. Jared was there, so I didn't get the one-on-one time with her that I preferred.

"Pretty uneventful."

I wondered what she did with Nathan. How often did she see him? Were they really hitting it off? I didn't ask her anything because I always regretted doing it in the past. Due to my jealousy, I couldn't be objective.

"Yours?"

"Same."

Silence stretched over the phone. I hated this distance between us. We missed each other but couldn't do anything about it.

"I'm going to Seattle on Sunday." I didn't have anything else interesting going on in my life. Just to break the silence, I blurted out the first thing that came to mind. "My brother is having surgery, so I'm taking over the office for him during the week."

"Oh…" Instead of asking a bunch of question, she seemed to be surprised.

"He didn't tell me until a few days ago. That's why I didn't mention it."

She finally found her voice. "Is he okay?"

"It's just a routine procedure. Nothing to be worried about. But, I agree he should stay home and get some rest. I don't mind taking over for him."

Austen was quiet again, her discomfort obvious through her silence.

"Everything alright, sweetheart?"

"Yeah," she said quickly.

"Is there something you wanted to talk about?"

"No. I just… Are you gonna see Rae?"

Now I understood why there was such an abrupt change in conversation. Just the way I was uncomfortable when Nathan was mentioned, she felt the same way toward Rae. "I wasn't planning on it."

"But doesn't she work there?"

"Yeah…but she works in the lab downstairs. I shouldn't have any reason to cross her path."

Austen had no right to be upset, but it was obvious she was. "Sweetheart, what's on your mind?"

"Nothing. I guess I'm just surprised. That's all."

"That I'm helping my brother?" I asked incredulously.

"No," she said quickly. "I just…never mind."

"No, tell me," I pressed. I knew Austen well enough to understand something was wrong. She could hide her feelings from anyone else, but not me. Even through a phone, I could pick up on her emotions. That's why our sex was so amazing. We were in tune with each other.

"It's nothing."

"Goddammit, Austen," I said with a growl. "Just spit it out. You're talking to me."

"I guess I'm jealous. That's all."

At least I wasn't alone. I got jealous too. "Nothing to be jealous of. Just going there for work. Nothing more."

"But you're going to see her and fall for her all over again. Trust me, I know. I do it with Nathan all the time."

I couldn't fall harder for Rae. The worst that could happen was that seeing Rae would prolong these feelings. As long as Zeke was in her life, my heart would never get its hopes up. "That's not gonna happen. Like I said, I'm not gonna see her."

"Maybe…"

We fell quiet again, sitting on the phone together but not speaking. The tension was still there, but there was nothing more to say about it. I'd never wanted someone so much that I couldn't have. We were divided by so many obstacles. "I wish I never left New York. I wish I met you before I met her." I didn't like to look back with regret, but my relationship with Rae hurt me far more than it made me happy. Everything could have turned out differently if I didn't fuck it up, but that didn't change the way I felt.

The softness had returned to her voice. "I know, Ryker. I wish I never met Nathan too."

The second I arrived in Seattle, I wanted to leave. It was cold, and it smelled like rain. It was nearly a hundred degrees in New York and painfully humid, but it felt like January on the other side of the country. I checked into my hotel and looked at the Space Needle from my bedroom window. I could see the same building from my old apartment and my old office.

It was strange.

Rae was probably at Zeke's house right now with their two dogs. Since it was Sunday, the gang was probably watching sports and playing board games. If the pavement wasn't so wet, they'd probably be playing ball at the courts.

The nostalgia was powerful.

I relaxed for the rest of the day before I woke up the following morning and went to work. I hadn't worn a suit in forever, so it was even more uncomfortable than usual. The tie was tight around my throat, and my dress shoes were stiff and shiny unlike my Nikes.

I walked into the building and couldn't help but think of Rae. What if I did accidentally run into her? What would I say? How would she look? When I arrived at my office, it was exactly the same…but different. My brother changed the pictures on the wall, the stationary on the desk, and the computer, but he didn't change the desk or the chair. When I spotted a picture of my father sitting on the corner, I shouldn't have been surprised.

I got down to work just the way I used to and was alarmed by how natural it was. I took phone calls like I owned the place and powered through annoying emails from different vendors. Time went by quickly, and I was relieved I would be out of there soon.

Sometimes, my mind would drift back to Austen. I wondered what she was doing back at home. I was three hours behind her, so by the time I got off work, she would be sitting on the couch drinking a glass of wine— possibly with Nathan.

I was just about to leave the office when someone stepped inside.

Rae.

She wore jeans and her old Nike sweatshirt. Her brown hair was pulled into a bun and she didn't wear any makeup. She was just as thin as I remembered, her neck slender. There wasn't a ring on her left finger, not that she would wear it to the lab. "Jen heard you were filling in, but I didn't believe her…"

I brushed off the encounter with a smile. "For once, the rumors are true." I pulled my satchel over my shoulder and came around the desk. Instead of hugging her like a normal person, I stayed a few feet back. It didn't feel right touching her, not after everything we'd been through—not when I felt like this. I vividly remembered the last time we slept together. She was depressed over Zeke, and it was just lustful sex. Now I understood how women felt when I used them to distract myself.

I felt like shit.

"That's awesome." Rae's face lit up in that beautiful and natural way. She didn't need to wear a skintight dress with makeup plastered all over her face to be beautiful. She had that natural look to her—just like Austen. "It's so nice to see you."

Maybe for her it was. "I'm leaving at the end of the week. My brother will be good as new by then."

"That was sweet of you to fill in for him."

I shrugged then stepped toward the door. "I'll see you later. Tell Safari I said hello." Even though that dog hated every time I went over there.

"Whoa, hold on." She stepped in my way even though she didn't have the size to block my path. "You wanna grab dinner or something? Everyone would love to see you."

I scoffed because that was so untrue it was hilarious. "Rex has made his feelings for me perfectly clear. And I don't blame Zeke for hating me as well. After all, I did try to steal you from him." I wasn't going to sugarcoat what I did. I wanted Rae back so much I was willing to sabotage her current relationship—a dick move.

"That's all in the past."

If someone tried to take my woman away from me, I wouldn't be quick to forget. "Rae, it's okay. I've got a lot of friends in the city that I can hang with. Don't worry about me."

"Who said anything about being worried?" she said. "Maybe I'm asking you to dinner because I actually want to talk to you? To hear about your life? I thought we were friends?" Once the hurt entered her voice, I actually felt bad.

"Of course, we're friends. But I don't think Zeke would appreciate us spending time together." I didn't need to remind her what happened last time the pair of us had dinner. He caught our affection and assumed Rae was leaving him for good. But he got the picture completely wrong. "I don't need to tell you that."

She crossed her arms over her chest, doing a pitiful job of looking menacing. "We don't need to worry about him."

I raised an eyebrow, knowing I wouldn't be okay with her having dinner with Zeke if our fate had turned out differently.

"He has nothing to worry about—and he knows it."

We walked into Mega Shake, and I inhaled the familiar scent of greasy fries. Rae and I had been there a few times, and the food never disappointed. We ordered our meals then sat across from each other in one of the old booths.

She sipped her milkshake, working hard to suck the heavy cream through the straw. Her cheeks hollowed, and her eyes focused on her straw.

I couldn't help but think of those excellent blow jobs she used to give me.

Get your head out of the gutter, Ryker.

She finally put the damn milkshake down and grabbed a handful of fries. "Does it feel weird being back at COLLECT?"

"Actually, no. Feels exactly the same, like nothing has changed."

"That's good."

"My brother didn't do much redecorating. Must've liked my style."

"Or he's just lazy like you," she teased.

"Yeah…that's more likely."

She grabbed her burger with both hands and took a big bite.

"How are Safari and Razor?"

"Both good. Safari is showing Razor the ropes. You know, the best pee spots in the backyard and where to find the bones in the flower garden."

E. L. TODD

I chuckled when the mental image filled my head. "Sounds like a good pair of friends."

"Safari doesn't pay much attention to me anymore," she said with a shrug. "But that's fine."

"Kids have to grow up sometime…"

She kept stuffing her mouth without breaking her strike. Rae was one of the guys, but she was more beautiful than all the girls. "How's life in New York?"

"It's okay." Austen was my entire life there. She made me feel less alone in that city of seven million people. "I work out a lot and play a lot of video games. Pretty boring."

"If you told Rex that, he'd be jealous."

I finally ate a few fries.

"So…" She set down her burger and leaned forward. "What's up with Austen? Did you tell her how you feel?"

"Actually, yes."

"And?" She leaned forward even more.

"She's still in love with her ex and is gonna give him another chance."

Rae's jaw dropped and nearly hit the table. "Are you serious?"

I shrugged and kept eating. "He's the love of her life."

"Is this woman stupid?" she hissed. "You're perfect, Ryker. Is she blind?"

I wasn't that perfect. If I were, Rae would have picked me.

"You didn't chase her?"

"I can't compete with a guy she was going to marry. I told her if she felt that strongly about him, she should give him another chance."

Her eyes narrowed. "So you let her go?"

"What was I supposed to do?"

"Fight for her, obviously."

It would have been an uphill battle. "I didn't have anything better to offer her. If she picked me, she may have regretted it down the road. She deserves a man's entire heart, not just a sliver of it." Rae knew I was still in love with her. I didn't need to remind her of that.

"But this guy cheated on her."

"She wants to give him another chance. That's how I know she's really into him." Rae took back Zeke after what he did. Rae wasn't the kind of woman to sweep something like that under the rug, but she loved him enough to forgive him. "It just wasn't meant to be."

"Nothing is meant to be. Love is tough. You have to work at it."

I sipped my soda and grabbed more fries. "What's new with the gang?"

She wouldn't let me change the subject. "Ryker, you do have a lot to offer this woman. I know you do."

"I don't." My heart was beating so fast just sitting across from Rae because she still got my blood pumping. Even in that old sweatshirt and a messy bun, I still thought she was beautiful. She was the first woman I ever loved. It would take me a long time to truly get over her. "That's not how I want to start a new relationship. Maybe one day it'll happen. But for now—"

"For now, you have an incredible woman that wants you as much as you want her."

How many times did I have to say it? "She's in love with her ex, Rae. And I'm in love with you. The timing simply isn't right."

Rae did a great job of hiding her reaction. "How are you supposed to fall in love again if you keep living in the past?"

"Maybe we should stop talking about this." I knew she was passionate about it because she wanted me to be happy. If I was, she would be guilt-free and could stop worrying about me. "It's not going to change anything."

Irritation crept into her features when she didn't get her way, but she controlled her tongue. "Just think about it, Ryker."

"Noted."

"Because I remember the way you talked about her... She doesn't seem like just any other girl."

She certainly wasn't. Austen was beautiful, smart, and funny. She could rock my world better than any other woman I'd been with. There was always something I didn't like about the women I went out with

—but I didn't have a single complaint about Austen. "She's not."

Rae gave me a sad look, wanting to fix my relationship just as she fixed everyone in the gang. She was a woman that wore her heart on her sleeve and loved everyone like family. Nothing would make her happier than seeing me happy. That was just the kind of person she was.

"How's Zeke's office going?" I didn't care about Zeke at all, but I wanted to change the course of this conversation. So far, all we'd talked about was me and her dogs.

"Good. His old assistant came back after maternity leave, and he's really happy to have her back."

"She runs a tight ship around there?"

"She's just a great assistant. Zeke says he always gets off work on time when she's around. But once he had to hire a temp, and he was always there an hour later than usual. He's much happier now."

I could imagine. If I had Rae waiting at home for me, I'd sprint out of the office too. "And how are the two lovebirds?"

"Rex and Kayden?" she asked with a chuckle. "Still shacked up together across the hall from my old apartment."

So Rae had moved in with Zeke. That's what I figured. "I'm glad they're still together."

"I think they're gonna be together for a long time." She crossed her fingers. "At least, I hope so."

"She's made an honest man out of him?"

Rae rolled her eyes. "She's made a *man* out of him."

I chuckled. "Good for him."

"You wanna come by the house. Everyone is coming over for the game anyway."

That was the most hostile place I could think of. I definitely wouldn't be welcome there. "Thanks for the invite, but I'll pass."

"Oh, come on. What else are you going to do tonight?"

I could always call up Monica. She seemed to be into me before I left. "Wild and crazy stuff."

She rolled her eyes. "I don't believe that for a second. Please, come over."

That sounded like a stupid idea to me. "Rex and Zeke aren't gonna be thrilled about that."

"They don't have a problem with you, Ryker."

I laughed sarcastically because it was ridiculous. "Sure…"

"They really don't. I'll prove it to you."

"How about you don't?"

She pointed her finger in my face. "You're coming over, and that's final. Hang out with us."

I used to be part of their little group. Honestly, I missed it. I had my own friends, but it wasn't the same.

We weren't as close as Rae was with everyone else. "If you really think it's a good idea…"

Rae opened the door and walked inside. She was greeting by barking from both of her dogs and some incoherent acknowledgement from the living room. "Hey, guys. Look who I ran into."

Rex spoke from the living room, which couldn't be seen from the entryway. "I hope it was the pizza guy because I'm starving."

Rae rolled her eyes and shut the door behind me. "Even better."

"The ice cream truck guy?" Rex asked with excitement.

Kayden's voice came next. "My boyfriend is an eight-year-old."

"Ooh…my lady is a pedophile," Rex said. "Kinda kinky."

Safari looked up at me but didn't seem to hate me like he used to. He wagged his tail then looked up at me with his tongue hanging out. Razor sniffed me, greeting me in a special dog way.

Zeke walked from the living room and through the kitchen to the entryway. When his eyes settled on me, he couldn't hide his surprise. He clearly hadn't been expecting me at all. But he didn't break his stride as he met me in the entryway. "Long time, no see." He extended his hand with genuine welcome on his face.

I hid my own surprise at his warm greeting and shook his hand. "Too long."

Rae smiled as she watched the exchange. "Ryker is filling in for his brother at the office. We got Mega Shake after work."

"Cool." If Zeke was jealous, he didn't show it. "You must miss that place."

"There's one in Manhattan, actually." There were only two in the country, and they both happened to be in cities that I frequented.

"Cool," he said. "I didn't know that." He wrapped his arm around Rae's waist and gave her a kiss. "Bring me a milkshake?"

"No," she answered. "I was gonna split mine with you...but I drank it all."

He smiled in a genuine way, like everything she said was heartwarming to him. Without saying he loved her, his feelings were written all over his face. "That's okay, baby. There's always next time."

"Shit, it's Ryker?" Rex whispered loudly from the living room.

I could tell Rex hadn't changed much.

Kayden came into the kitchen first and greeted me with a hug. "Hey, are you enjoying the rain already?"

I hugged her back, surprised by her niceness as well. "It's a nice break from Manhattan. It was a hundred degrees and humid when I left."

"Yuck," Kayden said. "Good thing you're here."

Rex came next, his eyebrows raised because he couldn't believe I was standing there. "Didn't expect to see you again."

Before I left, it seemed like Rex hated me more than anyone else. He never forgave me for what I did to his sister. In my heart, I knew I couldn't blame him. Rae was everything to him—even if he wouldn't admit it. "Ditto."

Rae stared him down.

Rex purposely ignored her.

To my surprise, Zeke nudged him in the side. "Come on, man. Bury the hatchet."

In that moment, I knew Zeke deserved Rae more than I ever did. He was the better man, by far.

Rex eyed his sister and Zeke before he dropped his hostility. He finally extended his hand. "It's good to see you, man."

I took his hand and finally felt welcome in the house. I didn't feel like the asshole that broke Rae's heart. Now I was a friend, a member of the group that came and went. "You too, Rex."

I lay in bed in my hotel room, thinking about texting Monica to see if she was still single. She was a good lay with a smoking body. It would be easy to get lost in her, to give in to the carnal passion a man and a woman could find in each other.

But I knew I really wanted Austen.

Now that I was alone, my thoughts turned back to her. I stared at my phone and waited for her to text me, even though I knew she never would. She was three hours ahead, so she fell asleep hours ago.

Hopefully, she fell asleep alone.

I knew I should leave her alone. I shouldn't text her just to ease my own loneliness. She was the closest thing I had to a best friend. Like Rae could tell Kayden and Jessie anything, that was how I felt about Austen.

I gave in to my weakness and sent her a message. *Awake, Stone Cold?*

To my surprise, the dots lit up immediately. *How's Seattle?*

Cold. Wish you were here to keep me warm. It was a stupid thing to say, but I missed her. For some reason, being around Rae made me miss Austen even more. Rae had Zeke, and Austen was the closest thing I had to someone special.

Wish you could bring me an ice cream to keep me cold.

I chuckled, knowing exactly how hot it was there. *I'd eat it before I got there.*

Then I would cry.

The story wasn't even real, and I somehow felt guilty. *Then I'll make sure I bring two.*

The three dots appeared immediately. We were typing so fast it seemed like the conversation was happening in real time. *How was your day?*

Crappy. I had to work.

Welcome to the real world. It sucks.

I'm catching on.

Did you see Rae?

A felt a jolt of excitement surge through me when I recognized her jealousy. *Actually, yeah. She heard I was in the building so she came by my office.*

Now the dots were gone.

I tried to think of something to say to improve the conversation. I didn't want to stop talking to her. *Are you alone tonight?*

The dots came back. *Yeah. Are you?*

It's just you and me.

I wished she was here and not on the other side of the country. She was seeing Nathan now, so I couldn't hope for any more nights together. But it was still nice to pretend that it could happen...in my personal thoughts.

How was your day? It didn't matter how trivial her afternoon was. It was interesting to me.

Good. I finally went to the gym.

Yeah? I smiled when I pictured her running on a treadmill. *How'd it go?*

I remembered how much I hate the gym. It's so hot, all the girls are dressed in their super cute workout clothes while I'm wearing my old MIT t-shirt, and the meat heads are more into themselves than the chicks.

Wow. I can feel your anger. Maybe you should try jogging outside or something.

In one hundred-degree weather?

At least you'll burn more calories.

Are you saying I need to burn more calories?

I grinned. *You know I think you're absolutely perfect. My dick thinks so too.*

The dots stopped.

I probably shouldn't have said that, but I didn't feel bad about it. It was the truth and we both knew it.

I took my stupidity to a new level. *Miss you.*

Three dots lit up the screen. *Miss you too.*

I loved seeing those words. I read them three times in a row.

When are you going to be home?

Next week.

What are you going to do to keep yourself busy?

Knowing Rae, she was going to force me to hang out with her and the gang. *Work. Eat. Gym.*

No video games?

I don't have my gear with me, unfortunately.

Well, I'm always here if you want to chit chat.

There was no one else I loved to chit chat with more.

Thanks. I'll keep that in mind. I'll let you go to sleep now. I know it's late.

Goodnight.

Goodnight, sweetheart.

4

AUSTEN

I was walking on my treadmill desk in my black dress and running shoes. The outfit clashed, but I couldn't wear heels on the machine, so I had to switch out my shoes. People could make fun of me all they wanted. I didn't care how goofy I looked.

"Austen?" Vanessa rapped her knuckles on the open door.

"What's up?" I kept my face forward and typed my email at the same time.

"A man named Nathan is here to see you. Wants to know if you want to get lunch."

My hand smacked against the stop button. "He's here? Right now?"

"In the lobby."

The adrenaline spiked in my chest, and I felt my hands shake. Nathan still made me nervous when he caught me off guard. Butterflies fluttered in my stomach and swirled around, making me tense and nauseous.

Vanessa continued to stand there. "So…what should I tell him?"

"Uh, tell him I'll be right there."

She left.

I shut my laptop and quickly grabbed my purse. I checked my face in my compact and realized my makeup still looked fresh and my hair wasn't a mess from being on the treadmill. I walked into the lobby and saw him sitting in one of the large white chairs.

He smiled when he saw me and stood up. "Glad you're free." His eyes left my face and moved downward until they fixated on my feet. One of his eyebrows raised, and he suppressed a smile. "Is this in style now or what?"

I looked down at my red running shoes, realizing I never took them off. "Oh shit. I'll be right back."

"It's fine," he said with a laugh. "I don't care. It's just an interesting choice."

I tried to hide my embarrassment. "I work on a treadmill desk, so I change into these throughout the workday."

"Oh, now it makes sense."

"I'll be right back." I darted back into my office,

feeling like a moron for forgetting something so critical. I slipped on my black heels and walked back out, feeling uncomfortable but looking nice.

Nathan eyed my shoes. "Those match a little better. But I think I prefer the others more."

"They are more comfortable." I adjusted my purse and we stepped into the elevator together.

"So, what are you in the mood for?"

"Anything, honestly."

"Tacos?"

"I could eat tacos anywhere, anytime." They were one of the greatest inventions of humanity.

"Me too."

We walked a few blocks before we entered the shop and ordered our food. We took a seat with our drinks, and they brought our trays a moment later.

Nathan only got two tacos and skipped the cheese and the sour cream, trying to watch his waistline.

I ordered four and didn't give a damn. I was surprised Ryker's dick liked my figure so much. "How's work?"

"Pretty good. We're working on a new IT logo for this company out of California. A winery."

"How'd it turn out?"

"When you have too many cooks in the kitchen, it's always a slow start. But we'll get there. What about you?"

"I'm trying to get a hold of this guy who went viral for choreographing a dance with his two bulldogs. I thought he could be a great indirect sponsor. People always go for the big advertisements, like newspapers and magazines. But since people know those are advertisements, they aren't as effective. It's gotta be subliminal."

"Like Coke or Pepsi?" he asked. "How they make you want a Coke rather than just convincing you to buy a Coke?"

"Exactly." Since Nathan and I were in the same line of work, we had something to talk about.

"Good thing I got a Pepsi today." He took a drink. "Now I'm really craving one."

"Man, I love soda. I only allow myself to have one a day…even though I usually slip."

"Life is short. Drink the soda." He tapped his Styrofoam cup against mine before he took a drink.

"You're very wise." Any excuse to drink an extra soda was a good one for me.

"I know," he said with a handsome smile.

I still loved those sparkling eyes and nice smile. He had a hard jaw lightly covered with hair, and I missed running my fingers across it as I kissed him. The longer I stared at him, the more I felt my attraction grow. When Nathan and I were together, I didn't just love him —I was infatuated with him.

Nathan caught my look and stared at me back. "What?"

Maybe I was making it obvious. "Nothing." I grabbed a taco and took a bite.

"You sure? You had this look on your face."

"I was thinking about how stupid I was for not changing out of my running shoes." Ryker would get a kick out of that when I told him later.

"I've done things much more embarrassing than that."

"I highly doubt it." Nathan was meticulous and a perfectionist. His physique could easily be carved out of marble with a chisel. His apartment had always been spotless. He knew exactly how much money he had in his bank account at any given time. "Give me something specific."

"Uh…can't think of anything off the top of my head."

"Trust me, if you did something really embarrassing, you would remember it."

"Alright." He smiled. "I was just trying to make you feel better. You caught me."

"I knew it." I shook my head before I kept eating.

He finished one of his tacos then wiped his hands with a napkin. "Are you free tonight?"

I was free almost every night. Madeline was tied up with Liam now, and Ryker and I weren't seeing each other anymore. Jared was single now, so I could always hang out with him. We could have a hot wing eating contest, which we'd done many times. "Yeah. Got any ideas?"

"How about we get dinner and watch a movie?"

That was definitely a romantic date. I said I would give Nathan another chance, but we'd only hung out here and there. We never really had a true date. Everything had been casual since our situation was so strained. I had no reason not to say yes, so I went for it. "Sure."

He didn't smile, but his eyes showed his excitement. "Great. I'll make the reservations."

"Good. I'm not much of a planner."

He chuckled. "I remember."

We ordered a bottle of wine and made small talk over candlelight. The place was fancy for a mid-week meal, but I didn't make any jokes about it. Nathan wanted to take me somewhere nice, and I wouldn't tease him about it.

He looked good in his collared shirt and slacks. It fit tightly across his shoulders and waist, showing the musculature. Ryker's body was similar, packed with lean and tight muscle, but Nathan was a little thicker. I shouldn't compare the two men, but it was difficult not to.

The thought of Ryker made me wonder if he was hanging out with Rae again. I was jealous of a woman I'd never met, and I shouldn't be. She picked someone else over him, so she was clearly a moron. I shouldn't care in the least.

But I did.

Nathan stared at me from across the table, looking devilishly handsome now that he shaved his face. He got his rugged good looks from his father and his pretty eyes from his mother. I could see his features in both of their faces. I wondered how they would react if they knew we were seeing each other again. They seemed to like me when I was dating their son, but I wasn't sure if that had changed.

"What are you thinking about?" he asked.

"Uh…your parents." I chuckled because the response was just as weird as it sounded.

"Well, whatever does it for you."

"I was thinking about how handsome you look, and I remembered you look a lot like your parents."

He smiled. "Well, thank you. I think you look like your mom, just a lot prettier."

I felt my chest tighten at the compliment, the air leaving my lungs. He still made my heart soar no matter what kind of compliment he gave me. "Thanks…"

My phone vibrated in my purse from the chair next to me. I heard it shake against the wood and noticed the light that came on in my peripheral vision. It was rude to look at your phone on a date, so I ignored it.

But I did wonder if it was Ryker.

Nathan and I talked about the marathon he was running in a few weeks and how much money he'd raised for charity. He had a big heart when it came to things like that. It made me wonder how he got so mixed up with Lily in the first place since it didn't match his personality at all.

My phone vibrated again.

It probably was Ryker, wondering what I was doing tonight. Last night, I lay in bed at one in the morning and continued to talk to him. I was exhausted, but I couldn't close my eyes and end the conversation. No matter what the subject was, I wanted us to keep talking.

Our dinner was brought a moment later, and my phone vibrated again.

This time, Nathan said something. "I'm not going to be offended if you check your phone."

Since he noticed, I was obviously distracted enough that I may as well look. I opened my clutch and pulled out my phone.

All the messages were from Ryker.

What are you doing?

He sent a picture of him and his mom at the harbor.

She had the same dark brown hair and the same colored eyes, but that was the only features they had in common. It was ironic that Nathan and I were just talking about our parents, and Ryker was hanging out with his. *I took my mom to dinner.*

My eyes softened as I looked at the picture, seeing the soft side of Ryker that he hardly ever showed. Something about him hanging out with his mom was adorable.

Are you at the gym? He inserted a happy face.

I wanted to write back but I knew I shouldn't. I would get in the middle of a long conversation that would never end. That would be really rude to Nathan, to talk to a guy I used to fool around with…and missed fooling around with.

"Everything okay?" Nathan asked.

"Yeah. People are just blowing up my phone with nonsense." I turned it on silent then placed it back in my clutch.

Nathan wasn't as playful as he was a moment ago. He drank his wine then looked away.

I wondered if he assumed it was Ryker.

Since it was him, I wouldn't deny it. That would be a lie. "This wine is good."

He cleared his throat. "Yeah…pretty good."

The moment I walked into his apartment, it felt like his personal space. The tones of gray and black fit his personality perfectly. Most of his furniture had been changed since he lived with me, so he must have redecorated at some point. "Your place is nice."

"Thanks." He walked into the kitchen and poured two glasses of wine. "Can I get you anything else? Popcorn?"

I rubbed my big stomach. "I'm so full."

"Maybe in ten minutes?" he teased.

I rolled my eyes and sat on the couch.

He sat beside me and placed the glasses on the table. "What movie do you want to watch?"

"You know I'm not picky."

"How about *Billy Madison*?"

He remembered that was my favorite movie. "You know I can't say no to a classic like that."

He smiled then turned it on. All the lights were off, so only the glow from the screen filled the apartment. He sat beside me and didn't touch me, but I was aware of how close we were to each other.

He placed his arm over the back of the couch, resting it against my neck. His skin was warm to the touch, and my breathing hitched slightly at his proximity. I crossed my legs and gripped my glass of wine by the stem.

I was so nervous.

I knew what was going to happen during the movie,

but I still felt anxiety. I'd kissed Nathan a million times, so I shouldn't be worried, but the butterflies in my stomach had grown to the size of dragons. Fire-breathing dragons.

Nathan didn't make his move right away. He gave me a false sense of security by watching the movie for thirty minutes and laughing at the best parts.

I sipped my wine and continued to grip it like a life preserver.

Eventually, Nathan pulled the glass from my hand and placed it on the coffee table.

I knew it was coming.

He leaned back again and turned his body so his hand could move into my hair. He moved slowly, but it felt like everything was passing at the speed of light. He leaned into me and pressed his mouth to mine.

It felt nice.

His lips were soft but strong, commanding my mouth with their power. His thumb brushed against my cheek as he kissed me slowly.

My mouth moved with his as my hand inched up his chest. I felt the strong muscles of his body and tightened my thighs together as the chemistry swept through me. He was just as great of a kisser as he'd always been.

He breathed into my mouth before he gave me some of his tongue. He was an excellent kisser, knowing exactly when to push and when to pull. He could feel my passion through his lips and gave me exactly what I craved.

He kissed me harder and dug his fingers into my hair, getting a strong grip on me. His tongue danced with mine and he breathed with me, our mutual arousal building and becoming stronger.

The movie was forgotten.

As much as I enjoyed the physical chemistry between us, I didn't want it to go any further than this. I wasn't ready to sleep together. It was too soon for that. I hoped Nathan realized that and didn't push things.

He guided me down to the couch and moved on top of me, his powerful frame suspended over me.

The movement was so fluid that I didn't stop it, but I didn't want it to lead to anything more serious. "Nathan—"

"I know." He broke our kiss and rubbed his nose against mine. "We'll take it slow."

5

RYKER

You wanna play ball with us? Rae texted me at the end of the workday.

I knew she would pester me to hang out with them, even though being around her was difficult for me. Zeke wasn't too far behind, so that made it worse.

When I didn't respond right away, she texted me again. *We're meeting at the courts right after work.*

I finally wrote her back. *I'll make the teams uneven.*

No, you'll make them even. Tobias likes to play. Jessie is getting really big and doesn't like to move much.

Damn, I walked right into that. *I already have plans.*

Shut up. If you don't show up, we'll come looking for you.

I knew better than to call her bluff. *Fine.*

Great! See you then.

I was spending my evenings with my ex, who I was still in love with, and her boyfriend. When did my life turn into this? Maybe I should just hang out with my mom again. I knew that would make her happy.

After work, I went home and changed then walked down to the basketball courts. I checked my messages and was a little hurt Austen never wrote me back. When I didn't see those dots light up the screen, I knew she was busy.

And she was probably busy with Nathan.

That was the worst part of all. If she was busy working late or hanging out with her friends, I wouldn't care. But knowing she was out with Nathan, or even worse, home with Nathan, made my stomach boil in acid.

I shouldn't care.

After all, I was the one who encouraged her to make it work with him.

Because I was a stupid idiot.

I was still in love with Rae, so I had my own problems.

But it still hurt.

I arrived at the courts and watched Rex make his practice shots. Kayden watched him with her arms crossed over her chest, clearly not into the sport like he was. She was only there because it made him happy.

The dogs were tied to the basketball pole, sitting up

with their ears perked with interest. Razor sniffed Safari's butt, and Safari growled at him so he would stop.

Rae talked to Zeke by the bench while she drank from her water bottle. She wore black leggings and a fitted top, her slender curves highlighted in the tight clothing.

I joined the gang. "Whose team am I on?"

When Rae saw me, she smiled like she was genuinely happy to see me. I used to get a different look from her all the time when she was in love with me. It made me sad to know I would never be the recipient of that look again—only Zeke would. "Depends. Has your game gotten rusty?"

"Never."

"I'm first captain." Rex tucked the ball under his arm.

"And I'll be second captain," Rae said.

"Why can't I be second captain?" Zeke asked as he joined us on the court.

"Because you're too slow to call it," Rae said. "So that's too bad."

Zeke rolled his eyes but smiled at the same time. "Whatever you say, baby."

"Alright," Rex said. "I call Zeke."

"Hey." Kayden put her hands on her hips. "You pick him over me?"

Rex shrugged. "That's life, sweetheart. Sorry."

"I'll make sure to say that to you later tonight," she snapped.

Tobias chuckled. "Ouch. If my lady wanted to play, I'd always pick her."

Rae went next. "I call Ryker."

"Ouch," Tobias said. "You think he's a better ball player than me?"

"He's better at three pointers than you are," Rae said. "That's just how it goes."

Rex went next. "I got Tobias."

Kayden stomped her foot. "So you don't want to be on my team at all?"

"Think about it this way," Rex said. "Now I can cover you." He winked.

Kayden rolled her eyes then walked over to Rae. "Jackass."

"If it makes you feel any better, Zeke isn't on my team either," Rae said.

She shot a glare at Rex. "It doesn't."

"Alright," Zeke said. "Let's play ball."

***

"I can't believe we got our asses kicked by two chicks." Rex shook his head as he dribbled the ball down the sidewalk to Mega Shake.

"I can," Zeke said. "Michael Jordan has nothing on Rae."

"Yeah whatever," Rex said. "She's such a showoff."

Rae walked in the front with me and didn't turn around. "I can hear you, you know."

Rex started talking louder. "I was hoping you could."

"You know, I was there too," I said. "Made a lot of good shots."

Rae rolled her eyes. "They just can't handle losing to a team with a chick on it. Rex is a sexist asshole like that."

"Am not," Rex called from the back.

We walked into Mega Shake and ordered our food before we sat down. I noticed Zeke and Rae didn't necessarily sit together or try to be close to one another. I wasn't sure if that was for my benefit or Rex's.

Rex sat beside Kayden, and when he placed his hand on her thigh, she swatted it away.

"What?" he asked.

"Don't touch me like you didn't just throw me under the bus back there." She picked at her fries.

"What bus?" Rex asked. "Look, when it comes to sports, I have to build the best team. How else am I going to beat Rae? I need to do it at least once."

"Instead of focusing on your team, maybe you should just suck less," Rae jabbed.

Zeke tried not to laugh, knowing he should remain objective between his girlfriend and best friend.

"I don't suck," Rex snapped. He shoved a handful of fries into his mouth. "You suck." His words could barely be understood because his mouth was so full.

Rae threw a fry at him. "I know Mom taught you some manners."

"Well, he forgot them all," Kayden said. "I'll have to put him back into training."

"Isn't there an obedience school just down the road?" I jabbed.

Rex's eyes narrowed at me. "They can talk shit. You can't, asshole."

I kept a stoic expression despite the way the insult stung.

"Rex." Kayden smacked his arm. "That was not okay."

Zeke shook his head. "That was low, man. We're all friends here. Let's move on."

"Thank you," Rae said to both of them. "I wish Rex shared our maturity."

Rex ate his burger, looking low now that he was outnumbered. "Sorry…I've always been weird about Rae."

"Yeah, I caught on to that," I said sarcastically.

Rex handed me his shake. "You wanna try mine? That's as good as an apology, right?"

I held up my hand. "Uh, I'll pass. But thanks for the offer."

Rex pulled it back and took a drink. "Are you seeing anyone in the big apple?"

"Kinda. A little. Not really." I was seeing a really awesome girl until I fucked that up.

Zeke was about to take a bite of his burger. "Wow… that's a complicated answer."

"You know me." I drank my soda. "I've always been the complicated type."

"So, what does that mean?" Rex asked. "Like, you aren't sure if you want to be in a relationship? I was like that with Kayden until I realized I couldn't live without her. Don't worry about keeping your junk on the market. When you find the right woman, you'll be glad she's the only one you're banging."

Kayden's eyes softened because she obviously thought that was sweet.

Rae looked at Zeke. "I'm so glad that's not how you express your feelings to me."

Zeke chuckled. "That makes two of us."

"So what's the deal?" Rex pressed.

Rae knew the truth, but I wasn't sure if I could tell them the same thing. "She's still hung up on her ex. The guy cheated on her and left her for her best friend. But then he came back, and she's not sure if she wants to be with him or not. So I bowed out."

"Oh…that's brutal." Rex gave me a look of pity, the one and only time he'd ever done such a thing. "Sorry, man."

"It's okay," I said. "If I'm gonna be with a woman, I don't want to settle for half her heart."

"That's totally fair," Kayden said. "You did the right thing."

"But I miss her a lot. I think about her all the time." The melancholy spread through me, making me confess things I wouldn't normally say out loud. "I texted her a few times last night, and she never responded…so I can only assume she was with *him*."

They all gave me sad looks, actually feeling bad for me.

I shouldn't have told them that at all.

Zeke was the first one to speak. "Sounds like you really like this girl."

I shrugged, downplaying the truth. "She's pretty cool."

"Do you have a picture?" Kayden asked.

I chuckled under my breath because my phone was full of nothing but her. "Yeah." I pulled out my phone from my pocket and searched through the images until I found a really good one of her. She probably wouldn't like me showing this picture to anyone, but I loved the way she looked in it. She was asleep beside me, but her mouth was slightly lifted in a smile like she was dreaming. Her eyelashes were dark and thick, and they contrasted against her ivory skin. Her shoulder was exposed because the sheets fell off her slightly. She was naked, but nothing could be seen in the picture except her neck and arm. I handed it to Kayden.

Kayden stared at the screen before she smiled. "Aww…" She handed it to Rae.

Rae stared at it for a long time, her eyes taking in every aspect of Austen. "Ryker, she's beautiful. Look at those cheekbones, those lips. You took this when she was sleeping?"

"Yeah," I answered. "She still doesn't know I took it."

Kayden handed the phone to Zeke. "Don't give that to Zeke. I don't want him to see her."

Zeke rolled his eyes, probably because her request was ridiculous. It didn't matter how beautiful Austen was. He had Rae, so nothing could possibly impress him.

Rex whispered under his breath. "Wow…" He felt Kayden's terrifying look and quickly changed his tune. "Those sheets look really nice." He handed the phone to Tobias so he wouldn't get himself into deeper trouble.

"Damn, she's fine."

I took the phone back and stuffed it into my pocket. "She's perfect, I know."

"Are you sure you can't make it work?" Rex asked. "Come on, you're rich and hot. You should be able to make her forget her ex. He's a cheater anyway. Cheaters

85

are assholes." When he realized how that statement would affect Zeke, he apologized. "I mean, not all. But you know, some of them…"

Zeke bowed his head and threw more fries into his mouth, doing his best to sidestep the awkward topic.

I tried to help him out. "I really like her, but since I still have feelings for Rae, it's just not fair to her." Like I suspected, that made everyone awkward, but for a very different reason. "We both like each other but we've got our baggage. It's not exactly romantic."

Kayden was about to throw a few fries into her mouth, but missed and dropped them on the table. Rex tried to hide his discomfort by taking a big gulp of his milkshake. Zeke seemed indifferent to what I said even though he had every right to be uncomfortable.

Rae was the only one who didn't seem unnerved by my admission.

I took the heat off Zeke, but now things were seriously tense. "So, that's my love life…"

"Honestly, that sounds pretty perfect to me," Rex said.

Did he not understand what I said? "Huh?"

"You're both trying to get over other people, right?" he asked. "I say keep sleeping together until you forget your exes. That's what most people do anyway."

"But she wants to make it work with her ex," I reminded him.

"You know what I would do?" Tobias said. "I'd make her want to work it out with me instead." He winked and sipped his milkshake.

"Yeah…that's what people keep telling me." Even though it was a lot more complicated than they made it seem.

"If Kayden was thinking about going back to her ex, I'd bang her until she couldn't move," Rex said.

Rae cringed. "I guess I'm done eating…"

"Like I don't have to see you and Zeke make out all the time," Rex snapped. "I can't count the number of times I've thrown up."

I kinda wanted to throw up right now.

"I'm just saying, don't be the loser," Rex said. "Woman like to be chased, to be pursued. If you chase her hard enough, she'll forget that other guy. You're hot stuff, so don't forget that."

That was the second time he called me that.

"Stop calling him hot," Zeke said. "It's weird."

"I'm not saying I think he's hot," Rex corrected. "I just know lots of women want to jump his bones. This woman isn't immune. I'm sure the other guy has nothing on you."

"It sounds like you think he's hot," Tobias jabbed.

"Actually, Nathan is a good-looking guy." I understood why Austen had fallen for him to begin with. If he'd never cheated on her, he'd seem like a stand-up guy. He hit the gym religiously, had his shit together, and was always polite even when he was being insulted.

Rex shook his head. "I'm sure you're—"

"Hotter?" Zeke finished.

Rex nudged him in the side. "I was gonna say better."

Tobias rolled his eyes then ate a fry. "Sure you were."

I finished half of my burger then cut myself off. I couldn't eat like this all the time or I wouldn't keep my body fat below seven percent. And let's face it, women liked it that way.

"I have an idea," Kayden said. "What if we help you?"

"Help me?" I asked, having no idea how she could accomplish such a thing.

"What's that mean?" Rex asked. "He knows how to get pussy just fine."

"I mean, what if we come to New York and help," Kayden said. "We could have one of us lure this guy away from her so you could have Austen all to yourself."

That was the last thing I wanted to do. "If I did that, it would hurt her. And I would never, ever hurt her."

Kayden's eyes softened.

Rae patted me on the back. "We're sorry, Ryker. We all wish things could be different for you."

I believed her. I had my beef with Zeke and Rex, but they seemed to accepted me now. Their group was tight and cohesive, and they always fought each other's battles. I was more honest with them than my own friends in New York. "I know."

———

Out of principle, I refused to text her.

She never texted me back.

But I wanted to talk to her. I missed her. My dick was hard for only one woman. I was still tempted to call Monica or pick up someone from a bar, but that would just make me feel worse. It would stop me from thinking about that beautiful brunette, but only for so long. Once I was finished, she would flood back into my mind.

I lay in bed and looked out the floor-to-ceiling window to see the Seattle lights blanketed across the city. It was oddly similar to the view from my apartment in New York. My phone lay on my bare chest, the screen dark.

Don't text her.

Don't fucking do it.

Go to sleep.

I closed my eyes and tried to think about work, something that usually put me right to sleep because it was so boring. But my mind kept drifting back to the woman who stole my focus. Even though I was in the same city as Rae and spending time with her, I wasn't thinking about her as much as I thought I would. Seeing her with Zeke didn't kill me inside like I expected.

Fuck it, I'm going for it.

I opened her message app and typed. *It hasn't stopped raining since I got here. I actually miss the heat.* It was a stupid opener, and I knew it. But I wasn't on my game lately.

The three dots didn't appear.

Maybe she was already asleep. When she looked at her messages in the morning, she would just think I was pathetic.

As she should.

My phone lit up and began to ring.

Austen was calling me.

I stared at the screen and cleared my throat. I answered with a deep voice, trying to seem casual when I was only worked up. "Hey, Stone Cold. Hope I didn't wake you."

"No. I was playing Tetris on my phone."

"Tetris, huh?" She was such a nerd, but I loved it. "Are you any good?"

"I'm badass, actually."

"Yeah?" I was miserable a second ago, but now I was smiling. "You'll have to show me."

"I'll play you."

"I accept your challenge."

"Hope you aren't a sore loser," she said with a smile in her voice.

If she was the one beating me, then never. "I'm not sure. I always win." Except in the case of both Rae and Austen.

"So humble," she said sarcastically.

"We both know I'm a cocky asshole."

"At least you're honest about it."

I chuckled into the phone then listened to the static over the line. If I was quiet enough, I could hear her breathe. It felt like she was right next to me, sharing my big bed and making me feel less alone.

"Sorry I didn't text you back yesterday." Her voice turned quiet, heavy with guilt. "I just—"

"You don't have to explain anything to me." Actually, I wanted to know if she was with Nathan. Did they sleep together? Was she too busy sticking her tongue down his throat to text me back?

Jealousy was not a good color on me.

"I just didn't want you to think I was ignoring you."

"I'm too obnoxious to ignore."

"You've never been obnoxious," she said with a laugh.

"Really? Then we haven't spent enough time together." I wish we could spend more time together. I wish she were there with me now, or I was there with her. My cock hardened the longer I spoke to her, wishing he could be buried between her thighs.

She fell quiet, sitting in comfortable silence with me over the phone.

It was like having a quiet evening with your partner in the living room. The fire roared in the hearth and some random show was on the TV. There was no need to talk because silence was just as good as a great conversation.

I knew she was seeing Nathan, but I couldn't let her go. The only reason why she wouldn't have texted me last night was because he occupied her bed. But even then, I felt like I had a hold on her. "Were you with Nathan last night?" I shouldn't have asked. I was just torturing myself.

She hesitated before she answered. "Yeah…"

I closed my eyes and my ran fingers through my hair. The truth was a death blow, and I thought I could take it better than I did. I guess some pills were just too big to swallow.

"We had dinner then watched a movie."

Details I didn't need to know.

"I didn't sleep with him."

She didn't? My eyes snapped open and all the despair disappeared.

"We kissed on the couch…and then I went home."

I didn't like that part, but it was still better than them getting naked on the sheets. If she expected me to say something, she was going to be disappointed. I couldn't think of a single response.

"Have you met anyone over there?"

"Yes. A woman stayed over last night." I lied automatically, doing whatever I could to make myself feel better.

"Ooh…"

The second I heard the sadness in her voice, I felt terrible. Trying to make myself feel better made her feel worse. "Actually, I made that up. I'm sorry."

"Why did you lie?"

"Just wanted to make myself feel better. But it just made me feel worse instead."

When she sighed into the phone, I wondered if her breath was full of relief.

"I haven't been with anyone. It's hard to picture myself with anyone when I know how we feel about each other."

"I know what you mean."

My hand moved under the sheets, and I grabbed my length. My thumb brushed over my head and streaked the drop down my length. I closed my eyes and pictured Austen there with me, her perky tits right in my face while she rode me. "I wish I could be with you tonight…" I pictured her tongue licking over my length just the way my thumb did. My hand began to stroke up and down and my balls tightened at the touch.

"Me too."

I would give anything for everything to be different. I would give anything for Rae and I to never have crossed paths. Or better yet, I would give anything to be totally over her right now.

Anything at all.

6

———————————

RYKER

The week passed quickly, and I was back in New York.

Where it was hot as hell.

The second I returned to my apartment, I considered calling Austen. She knew I was coming back soon, but I didn't know if she knew I was back in town today. But even if she did, I shouldn't expect her to care.

Why did I continue to expect anything?

Liam texted me. *Yo, are you back in town?*

Just walked in the door.

Sweet. You wanna get food?

Maybe hanging out with Liam would cheer me up. *Sure. Where do you want me to meet you?*

At Riot. The game is on.

See you there.

I hopped in the shower and changed into jeans and a t-shirt before I walked down to the bar. When I reached the front, I spotted Liam standing outside with Madeline.

I didn't realize he was bringing her along.

"Hey." I fist-bumped Liam then hugged Madeline. "What's up?"

"How was your trip?" Liam asked.

"Pretty good. Saw my mom, and my brother is doing well. But I'm not a big fan of working."

Liam rolled his eyes. "I really hate you sometimes."

We walked inside and searched for a table. We took a seat and waved down the bartender and ordered our drinks.

"So did you do anything else there?" Liam asked. "Pick up some ladies?"

The question made me feel like a jerk even though I didn't have a girlfriend. "No." I didn't make eye contact with Madeline since she was Austen's best friend. "But I saw Rae, my ex. We hung out most of the time."

"And her current boyfriend was cool with that?" Liam asked incredulously.

"He was there too. We used to be friends."

The waitress brought the drinks and made unnecessary eye contact with me. She'd wanted to ask me out for a while, but I was never interested. They were all the same. We flirted, I took them back to my apartment, we had great sex, and then they were gone. After a few months, I would forget the incident altogether.

Liam stared at me harder than he ever had before. "Everything alright, man?"

"Yeah, I'm fine." I took a drink of my beer. "Why?"

"You just seem…" He tried to find the right word to describe my visage. "Sad."

I wasn't sad. I was miserable. "I had a long plane ride. Takes me awhile to get back on my feet."

Liam wasn't buying it. "It's because Austen is seeing Nathan again, huh?"

I averted my gaze and looked at the TV, unsure how to dodge the question.

"Because we aren't fans of the whole thing either." It was the first time Madeline jumped into the conversation. Liam had his arm around her shoulder, and she was cozied up into his side. "He really messed up, no matter how Austen justifies it. I'm not sure how she can forgive him."

"And you know I'll always hate the guy," Liam added.

Was this their way of making me feel better? "I'm happy for Austen. If this is what she wants, I support her."

Madeline shook her head, her lips pressed tightly together. "She wants you. I know she does."

My fingers suddenly felt numb. "She said that?"

"When she told me she had feelings for you, it seemed pretty intense. It seemed like more than just physical attraction or lust. There's a connection between you two. She feels it and so do you."

I drank my beer again, unable to believe I was having this conversation with Austen's brother and best friend.

"And I think you're miserable without her, even if you're still into this other chick," Liam said.

So everyone knew how hung up I was. "She told me she wants to make it work with Nathan."

"If she's gonna give him another chance, she should give you a chance," Madeline said. "I know how she feels about you. You guys are two peas in a pod. You're best friends. We see it. Don't you?"

I definitely saw it. "Are you guys telling me to fight for her or something?"

"Duh," Liam said. "I think that's obvious."

Maybe everyone was right. Maybe we should give this a chance even if we were still into other people. It wasn't like we were lying to each other. If we gave it another chance, maybe we would forget about Rae and Nathan and find what we needed in each other. "Maybe you're right. Maybe I should—"

I spotted Austen walk inside with Nathan by her side. Jared was there too, with a woman I'd never seen before. Nathan moved his arm around Austen's waist and guided her forward. They hadn't seen us yet, and Austen didn't seem to mind his affection.

I felt like shit.

Liam sighed and exchanged a look with Madeline.

They came closer to us and spotted us at the table. Austen stopped when she saw me, her eyes getting wide now that she'd been caught with Nathan on her arm. Nathan didn't drop his embrace, and I'm sure that was on purpose.

Jared was the first one to say something to break the ice. "You guys watching the game too?"

I couldn't even put on a polite face. Austen knew I was miserable, and so did everyone else. Why hide it?

"Yeah," Madeline answered. "You guys wanna join us?"

I'm sure Jared didn't want to see Madeline with Liam, and I obviously didn't want to see Austen linked to Nathan, but we couldn't say no.

"Uh, sure," Austen said. Nathan pulled out a chair for her and she sat down.

Like he was some kind of gentleman.

Could I really do this? Sit here and pretend everything was A-Okay?

It was awkward.

Like, really awkward.

Nathan was tense. Jared was uncomfortable. Liam drank half of his glass just to have something to do.

Austen stared straight ahead, not making eye contact with anyone.

It sucked.

I lost Rae because I didn't fight for her soon enough. I waited too long and missed my chance. Now there was another incredible woman in my life, one of a kind, and she was amazing. But I was letting this fuck up have her. He could have had her for the rest of his life, but he chose to fuck her best friend.

He chose to hurt her.

I couldn't repeat the same mistakes.

I couldn't live with the same regrets.

Fuck that.

"Austen, let's talk outside." I left the table and walked to the front without checking to see if she was behind me. I moved past the people huddled in the doorway and finally got to the humid air outside. It was hot and uncomfortable, but it was much better than sitting at the table with that douchebag.

When I turned around, Austen was there like I hoped. "I didn't know you were back in town—"

"I know I still have a thing for Rae and you still have a thing for Nathan. But you know what? Fuck them. We're great together, and I think we should give it a chance. Will it be perfect? No. Will it be normal? Probably not. All I know is, when I'm not with you, I miss you. And when you're with him, it kills me. He had his chance and screwed it up when he slept with Lily. Now give me a chance." I didn't think any of this through before I blurted everything out, but maybe that was a good thing. Maybe I was spending too much time thinking and less time doing.

People passed us on the sidewalk, paying no attention to our deep conversation and looks of consternation. Austen's eyes shifted back and forth as she looked up into my face, obviously unprepared for the bomb I just dropped on her. She walked into that bar expecting to have a normal evening with Jared and Nathan, and then she ran into me instead.

I would have felt awkward too.

"You want to give this a try?" she finally said.

"I can make you get over Nathan. You can help me get over Rae. Sounds perfect to me. There'll be lots of sex, and you know I'm always on board with that."

She crossed her arms over her chest, which wasn't a good sign. "When you were in Seattle, I was jealous the whole time. Jealous of what? I don't know."

"When you didn't text me back when you were out with Nathan, I went insane. I know exactly what made me jealous. Obviously, this thing between us is more than just a fling. You're my best friend, Austen."

Her eyes softened. "You're my best friend too…"

"So, what do you say?" I needed her to tell Nathan it was over once and for all. I wanted her to forget about him and stay with me. I had my baggage, but at least I was honest and faithful. Nathan had his chance, but he blew it. If she didn't pick me…it would hurt. I wasn't sure if I could handle that kind of rejection.

She eyed the door to the bar then turned back to me, torn between the two of us.

I was losing her. "I know you think he's the love of your life. Maybe he was at one point. But I can replace him. I can be the next man you can't live without. You just need to be a little patient with me. That's all."

"Ryker, I already said I would give him a chance…"

"And he already said he would spend the rest of his life with you. Then he fucked your best friend." That was low, and I knew it. I shouldn't use such a harsh tactic to get what I wanted, but I couldn't let her slip away. I should have fought for her in the first place. Only when I realized how much I needed her did I actually do something about it.

Just like with Rae.

Austen couldn't hide the hurt in her eyes. Nathan's betrayal would always be a sore spot for her. "I've forgiven him. No matter what happens with us, I've let it go. Holding on to the past like that wasn't healthy for me."

It was a jackass move to rub it in her face. "But he did mess up, Austen. I haven't."

"You slept with Cheyenne," she snapped.

"That was because I saw you kiss Nathan—"

"Kiss—that's all. I've spent a lot of time with him, and I still haven't slept with him. You jumped into bed with someone immediately. It hurt, Ryker."

That was a mistake that never should have happened. "I know…"

"You've both hurt me, Ryker. It took me forever to put myself back together after Nathan left. And even then…I've never been the same." She refused to have a relationship with anyone, choosing to have meaningless sex with random guys. I wasn't any different. "And then you hurt me again, which only reminded me why I swore off relationships to begin with."

"In my defense, we weren't in a relationship. And I already told you why I did what I did. Cut me some slack."

She shifted her weight, her eyes averted.

The distance was growing between us. "You can't honestly want to be with him over me."

"I never said that."

"Then why aren't you jumping into my arms right now? I thought we both agreed that we wanted each other."

"It's more complicated than that. If Nathan weren't in the picture, things would be different."

Why did that piece of shit have to apologize to her and try to win her back? "Fine. You're giving him a chance. But I want the same chance—at the same time." I stepped toward her, closing the distance between us. "That's fair, right?"

"What are you saying? You want me to date both of you and then choose?"

"Yeah." It was time to put on my armor and shield. It was time to go into battle and fight. "That's exactly what I want you to do. Date both of us for thirty days and then pick."

Austen stared at me incredulously until she realized I was being serious. "You aren't joking…"

"Do I look like I'm joking?"

"This was never supposed to be a competition."

"Well, it is now. And I'm gonna win."

"I doubt Nathan will be okay with that."

"That's too damn bad. If he doesn't like it, he can bow out. But I can promise he won't step away. He'll agree to the terms because he knows he has to play the game. He fucked up, and he has to prove himself. I have to prove myself too."

Austen tucked her hair behind her ear then stepped to the side when a guy almost brushed his arm against hers. "Uh…I don't know what to say."

"There's only one rule. You can't sleep with either of us." While I'd like to win her over with just my skills in the sack, I didn't want to share Austen in that way. "Everything else is fair game."

Nathan must have gotten impatient waiting for her because he came outside and joined us. He gave me a cold look before he came to her side. "Just wanted to see if everything was okay."

"She's fine." I needed to be civil to this guy because Austen cared about him, just as I knew she would be civil to Rae if they were ever in the same room together. "But she has something to tell you."

Her eyes widened when she understood my meaning. "Right now—"

"Yes, right now," I commanded. "Unless you've already made up your mind." There was no way she would walk away from me forever right on the spot. She missed me too much, confided in me too much. I meant just as much to her as she meant to me.

Austen looked at Nathan, the look in her eyes different. She wasn't nearly as comfortable with him as she was with me. She was a little more guarded, a little more uneasy. I could see it in the way her body tightened when she was close to him. "I'm going to date both of you for thirty days. At the end of that period, I'm going to pick one of you...because I can't pick right this second. It was Ryker's idea." She put the blame on me like I was the one causing the problem. If she would just forget this loser and choose me, we wouldn't have to go through with this.

Nathan eyed me again, his expression unreadable

now that Austen was looking right at him. He turned his expression back to her. "Is that what you want?"

Austen shrugged. "Ryker wants to be with me, and so do you. I'm not sure what I want right now…because I have feelings for both of you."

Nathan put his hands on his hips and did his best to hide his disappointment.

I hoped he would just give up and walk away. It would make my life a lot easier.

"I won't sleep with either one of you…that's the one rule," Austen continued. "But I understand if this is too weird or—"

"I'm in," Nathan said quickly.

Damn.

Austen eyed us back and forth, clearly uncomfortable that she had two guys openly competing for her.

I was up for the challenge.

"Okay…" She fidgeted with her hair awkwardly. "I guess that's what we'll do then."

"Fine with me." I gave Nathan an intimidating gaze, telling him he was going to go down hard.

"Yeah," Nathan said. "Let's do it."

"Well, since I was with Nathan tonight, I'll go back inside with him." Austen walked toward him but kept her hands to herself, not touching him in front of me.

Now I had to back off and play by the rules. "Are you free tomorrow?"

"Yeah, I think so," Austen said quietly.

"You aren't free anymore." I placed my hands in my pocket and walked away, knowing I needed to disappear for the evening. I couldn't go back in there and pretend I was okay witnessing them together.

I wasn't okay at all.

Now I was at war with Nathan, fighting over a woman like she was newfound territory. But I wasn't worried about losing her.

Failure wasn't an option.

I called Rae, and she picked up almost immediately.

"Miss the rain already?" she teased.

I chuckled because I couldn't disagree more. "No. I missed the sun."

"Yuck. If it's over seventy degrees, I get cranky."

Both places were beautiful and had their special qualities. I loved New York because of the nightlife, the chaotic beauty. I loved Seattle because it was laid back and mellow. The differences in weather were extreme, but that was okay.

"So, what's up?" she asked.

"I wanted to tell you that I decided to fight for Austen."

"Really?" Her smile leaked over the phone. "I'm so glad you changed your mind."

"I saw her with Nathan...and I got jealous."

"People say jealousy is bad. But I think it's pretty handy sometimes. What did she say?"

"She said she wasn't sure." I swallowed my pride at her answer. I shouldn't have expected Austen to jump into my arms right away. She'd been hung up on Nathan for years. She pictured him as her husband and intended to raise a family with him. It was hard for me to compete with that. "So I asked her to date both of us for thirty days and then decide."

"Man, that sounds like a great competition," she said with a laugh. "Two hot guys trying to win her heart... good for her."

My face contorted in a glare even though she couldn't see me.

She obviously felt it though. "Just in general..."

I brushed it off. "Neither one of us are allowed to sleep with her. So I have to win her over in some other way."

"You're an amazing kisser, Ryker. You've got this in the bag."

I automatically smiled when she stroked my ego. "Thanks. But I think I'm gonna need more than that."

"Just be yourself. You're a great guy, Ryker. Don't worry about it."

I obviously wasn't better than Zeke, and I may not be better than Nathan. "I'm afraid I waited too long. When I thought she was seeing him before, I hooked up with some woman and hurt her... The damage might be irreparable."

"Nothing is irreparable. You weren't seeing each other then, so it doesn't count."

That didn't mean it didn't hurt.

"I bet this guy is gonna do cheesy, romantic crap." Safari and Razor barked in the background, and Rae opened the door to let them outside in the backyard.

"Isn't that a good thing?"

"Hell no. Trust me, women want real shit."

"Real shit?" I asked incredulously.

"Yeah. I'm gonna tell you a really special secret, Ryker. All women want a man that gives them amazing sex. But they also want that man to be their best friend. Very simple. So skip the fancy dinners and moonlight walks on the beach. Take her to a baseball game and split a chili dog. Then rock her world when you get home. Watch one of those terrible Sci-Fi movies and make fun of it while you drink a few beers. Then go down on her like you haven't eaten all day. I'm telling you, it'll work."

I suspected this description derived from her

relationship with Zeke. I'd seen them together, and I knew that's exactly how their relationship was. They played a tough game of basketball, got burgers and fries, and then headed home to play behind closed doors. Rae and I never had a relationship quite like that. It was more intense, heavily based on sex and little else. It could have been much different if I just let her in.

But I didn't.

I let Austen in a lot more, and now I had to do even better. There was something about her that forced my walls to come down. I was pretty certain I had the exact same effect on her. We'd only known each other for a short period of time, but it somehow felt like forever. "I'll take your advice."

"Good. It can't do you wrong."

"Better not. I can't let this guy win."

"He doesn't deserve to win, Ryker. You're by far the better man."

"You haven't met the guy." I was totally straight, but I couldn't ignore his good looks. He had a solid build, a chiseled jawline, and handsome eyes. He was a serious competitor in the looks department.

"I don't need to meet the guy. What he did to her was just wrong. She never should have forgiven him in the first place."

I thought her statement was pretty ironic.

She must have read my mind because she said. "What

happened with Zeke was totally different. This guy cheated on her with her best friend and then kept doing it behind her back. He never came clean about it. You shouldn't judge a man based on his mistakes, but on his honesty."

"You sound like a fortune cookie right now."

"Shut up, jackass," she said with a laugh. "I'm trying to help you."

"I need all the help I can get for this one." If I lost Austen, I would never find anyone else again. It was a miracle I met another incredible woman after I lost Rae. It was one in a million that would happen once, but twice? It definitely wouldn't happen a third time.

I had to win.

"Maybe I can talk to her. You know, woman to woman."

That wouldn't do any good. "She's insanely jealous of you."

Rae took a moment before she could respond. "Of me?" she asked in surprise. "Are you serious? I live with my boyfriend and two dogs. I dress like a bum at work, and I can't cook for shit."

"She doesn't care about that."

"I've seen this girl. I've got nothing on her in the looks department."

Rae was beautiful, but Austen definitely had unique qualities. I loved her little nose, her beautiful eyes, and those soft cheeks. Not to mention, her body was unbelievable. "As long as I still have feelings for you, she'll always be jealous. I don't blame her. I feel the same way about Nathan."

Rae side-stepped the awkward topic and moved on. "You won't have feelings for me much longer. They'll fade quickly. It took me about four months to get over you, and you're almost there."

I'd never forget the way I broke her heart. I knew the aftermath was deadly. She was depressed for months, but she still had enough love in her heart to come to my father's funeral. I didn't know anyone else who would have the strength to do that. "We'll see."

"You can do it, Ryker. With a woman like that in your life, you'll forget all about me soon enough."

7

AUSTEN

Nathan walked me home with his hands shoved into his front pockets. We hadn't said more than two words to each other after my conversation with Ryker outside. It was one of the tensest moments we ever shared.

We entered my building then took the stairs to my floor.

Still no conversation.

When we arrived at my door, there was no other option but to face each other.

To look at each other.

Nathan made eye contact with me, and the annoyance was hidden deep inside his gaze. He did his best to hide it, but there was no way to mask his feelings. His shoulders were tenser than usual, and he lacked conversation. "That was a good game."

"Yeah...pretty close too."

He looked down the hallway even though there was nothing to look for.

As much as we didn't want to talk about this, we had to. "You wanna come inside?"

He slightly raised his eyebrows and pulled his hands from his pockets. "Sure."

I got the door unlocked, and we took a seat on the couch. Nathan sat on one end, and I sat on the other.

"I'm sorry about tonight. I didn't know he would be there."

"You don't need to apologize," he said. "I know he's still present in your life. I probably would have gotten just as jealous if I saw you with him."

I felt like an adulteress juggling two guys at once like this. I hardly ever had one great guy in my life, but now I had two. "If you don't want to do this, I wouldn't blame you." I wasn't sure if I'd have the confidence to fight for a guy when another woman was doing the exact same thing.

"After what I did to you, I have no right to complain. It doesn't surprise me that some other guy has fallen in love with you."

"He's not in love with me." The detail didn't matter, but I felt the need to say it.

"Are you sure about that?" he said sarcastically. "Because men don't fight over women unless they're worth fighting for. And they're only worth fighting for if they can't live without them. And if he can't live without you… You see where my logic is going."

The possibility made me feel good, but then I felt guilty immediately afterward. I couldn't choose between two guys, so I wasn't worthy of those feelings if that's how he really felt. "I don't think so. I know we have something special, but I don't think his feelings exist on that level."

He shrugged. "Whatever you say. I wouldn't put myself in this situation unless that's how I felt."

Nathan just told me he loved me, and I wasn't sure how to swallow it. He already knew I was still in love with him, so it shouldn't come as a surprise.

"I'm just grateful you're giving me a chance at all… after what I did. I think we could have everything we were supposed to have if we make this work. That wedding at the Plaza…the house in Connecticut…everything."

I used to dream about those things all the time…until they were snatched away.

Nathan leaned back into the cushion then looked at me. "Again, I don't have anything to complain about. I'm just grateful I'm in the running at all." He scooted closer to me on the couch then draped his arm around my shoulders. Then he leaned in and gave me a soft kiss on the lips. His mouth was closed but the embrace was still full of the kind of heat that crept up the back of my neck. My fingers felt numb, and the electricity I used to feel was still there—just like it used to be.

"So, let me get this straight." Madeline sat across from me at The Muffin Girl with her scone and coffee in front of her. "Two gorgeous men are fighting to be with you, and they're okay with that?"

"It was Ryker's suggestion." I would never ask two men to compete like this. Lots of women dated two guys at once, but that was usually in private. They figured out which one they liked more and then dumped the other. But in this case, both men were aware of the situation.

"But still, that's crazy. I've never experienced anything like that."

I had to stop myself from snorting. Jared was madly in love with her, and she was totally blind to that fact. I knew Liam and Jared would fight to the death to be with her. "I'm not a fan of the idea, but when Ryker asked me to decide right then and there, I couldn't."

"Really?"

I shook my head.

"Because it seems like Ryker is pretty perfect…"

He was perfect in a lot of ways. He was gorgeous, obviously. He had his shit together. He was funny, smart, and knew the female anatomy pretty damn well. Other than the fact he'd been devastated with heartbreak, he didn't have a single flaw—except the fact he was in love with another woman. "Rae is still on his mind."

"And Nathan is on yours. I think it's perfect."

"But that's not exactly romantic."

"What are you talking about?" She picked at her muffin and popped a piece into her mouth. "You guys are going to bang each other so hard until you both stop thinking about your exes. Sounds awesome to me."

"Maybe if I didn't have this lingering hope for Nathan, it would be different."

Madeline tried to hide her annoyance at my response but she failed. "I'm trying not to be one of those judgmental friends who tells you what to do…but this doesn't make any sense to me. Nathan cheated —period."

I absolutely agreed. "I know."

"If you know, why are you bothering with him?"

It made me pathetic. It made me weak. I wasn't denying any of that. "I've never stopped loving him. For the past few years, I was still devastated over what

E. L. TODD

happened. When you fall in love like that…it's hard to move on. He's everything I've ever wanted and—"

"I think you're trying to chase that happiness you used to have. You know, before he left you. I think that's the last time you've ever been truly happy, so you're trying to recreate it. But he did leave. He did cheat. You can't go back in time, Austen." She kept her voice steady so she wouldn't sound so bossy. "I know I don't understand because I've never been in this situation. And I know how much you loved the guy. I'm not trying to make you feel bad or put you down, but I really think this Nathan thing is a mistake. I'm trying to be supportive, but it's difficult when I see a great guy like Ryker within reach. Maybe if you guys really gave it a chance, he could make you happier than you ever were with Nathan."

I doubted that. When we were engaged and everything was perfect, I was on top of the world. I couldn't wait to come home to Nathan.

"Besides, what will your parents say if you do take him back?"

They wouldn't be happy at all.

"And you know your friends aren't on board with it either."

"I appreciate your concern, Maddie. But I shouldn't make my decisions based on your approval." Her

118

opinion meant a lot to me, but I couldn't be logical when it came to love. I thought with my heart and not my brain.

"I get that. But I really think you'll regret not picking Ryker."

"Why?"

"I see you and Nathan starting over, but once that initial rush wears off, you'll realize nothing has changed. You'll miss Ryker and all the things he used to give you, but by then, it'll be too late. I just don't want you to make a mistake, that's all. You've already been hurt enough. I don't want you to experience any more pain."

I knew Madeline always had my best interest at heart. "I know. I have some time to think about it, so who knows what will happen."

Ryker invited me over for dinner, so I arrived at his door in a new dress I got that afternoon. I knew there would be no sex for the next thirty days, and the idea of going through such a long dry spell didn't sound appealing in the least.

He opened the door in just his sweatpants. "Hey, Stone Cold."

Was he trying to torture me? His body was nothing

but chiseled muscle. The grooves and lines were nothing but beautiful shadows. My fingers remembered exactly how his warm flesh used to feel. My tongue remembered how he used to taste. "Hey…" I couldn't think of anything better to say, not when he opened the door looking like that.

"Come on in. The pizza just arrived."

"Pizza?" I stepped inside and saw the box on the counter. I could smell the grease and the cheese.

"Yep. Pepperoni, just the way you like it."

"I thought you said that was too plain?"

He shrugged. "Plain has grown on me." He put two slices on the plate and handed it over. "What do you want to drink? I just picked up a six-pack of Coke."

"You know I can't turn down a soda."

He grinned in that handsome, charming way. It was the kind that reached his eyes, giving them a playful glow. "I know my lady very well." He grabbed a can from the fridge, not breaking his stride like the possessive comment he just made was acceptable.

Once we had our pizza and drinks, we sat on the couch. He usually had a beer, but this time, he opted for a Coke so we could match. "What are we watching?" Even when he sat down, his toned body still looked perfect. His gut didn't hang over like mine did. He didn't have any kind of gut at all.

"You know I'm easy to please."

He grinned like he took my words in a different way. He grabbed the remote and flipped through the channels. "There're no good games on. How about something goofy?"

"Goofy, huh?"

"How about Dumb and Dumber?"

"I love that movie. Who doesn't?"

"Not a single person." He put the movie on then ate his pizza beside me.

His shirtless body was distracting. "Do you always eat shirtless?"

"Only when I'm trying to impress you."

"You impress me with a shirt on too."

"But I'm in the middle of a war right now. I have to use all the big guns."

Nathan was just as sexy. Either one of them could be on a pin-up calendar. I'd dated a lot of average guys, but Nathan and Ryker were truly exceptional. "Well, your guns are very big."

"Too bad I can't show you my biggest one." He kept eating like he didn't just mention his package.

"I've already seen it... I know it's big." When I thought about Ryker naked, it curbed my appetite and made me think about things I shouldn't. We weren't supposed to have sex, so I couldn't let my mind stray down that path. My legs needed to be locked together.

Ryker finished his pizza and tossed the plate on the

coffee table. His arm moved around my shoulders, and he moved close to me on the couch. He turned his head and looked down at me, the smell of his after shave coming into my nose. A slight smile was on his lips. "How was your day?"

"Good. I tripped in the break room and splashed coffee all over myself."

He chuckled. "And you classify that as a good day?"

"I had an extra sweatshirt in my office, so I just pulled that on."

"Why did you trip?"

"I usually wear running shoes when I'm on my treadmill desk. But I changed into my heels and I wasn't used to them, so I tripped on the carpet and dropped my coffee cup."

He pulled me closer into him and pressed a kiss to my temple. "It happens to the best of us."

"Actually, I don't think it happens to anyone. I'm just clumsy sometimes."

"I've fallen a few times."

I eyed him incredulously.

"Okay, maybe I haven't. But I'm supposed to make you feel better about it. That's what friends do." His hand moved into my hair, and he gently played with the strands. His fingertips were warm, and they always touched me in the perfect way.

"I thought friends tease each other?"

"They do that too. But I'm hoping we can make out during this movie, so I'm on my best behavior."

I smiled when I wished I wouldn't, feeling his fingers still dig into me. "You know I'll make out with you even if you're a total jerk."

"Because I'm hot?"

"Because you're arrogant, but hot."

"Awesome." He leaned into me and gave me a spontaneous kiss. His coarse facial hair rubbed against my soft cheek, and I loved the rough way it brushed against me. When he shaved his face, he looked clean and handsome. But I liked the beard too, the rugged woodsmen look.

His kiss was just as passionate as it'd always been, but it felt different somehow. The way his mouth expressed his urgency was unbelievably sexy. He kissed me like I was the only woman in the world he wanted to be with. His fingers dug into my hair and he gently wrapped the strands around his fist so he had a good grip.

My hands automatically moved to his bare chest, that impressive body I loved to feel against mine. Now I wished we were in his bed, his naked and sweaty body right on top of mine. My hand reached his shoulder, and I pressed my fingertips into his skin, feeling the powerful muscle that shifted directly underneath. My lips trembled when I needed to take a breath. I didn't want to stop kissing him, even for a second, but I needed to breathe.

Ryker slowly lowered me onto the couch until my back hit the cushions. He separated my knees with his then pressed his body right against mine. His hard-on was defined through his sweatpants, and it dug right against my throbbing clitoris.

Why the hell did I agree to the no sex rule?

Ryker held his weight on his arms and slowly grinded against me, pressing his cock in the perfect spot to make me writhe.

My arms moved around his waist and under his back, and the sensual kiss he gave me turned my brain into mush. All my thoughts were physical and carnal. I missed having him between my legs, stretching me the way every man should stretch his woman. "Ryker…"

"Sweetheart, I love it when you say my name." He broke our kiss and rubbed his nose against mine, his intense expression burning right into me. He grinded into me harder, stimulating my clit like he knew exactly what he was doing.

I was going to come.

I was dry-humping like a teenager, and I was actually going to come.

Ryker was either a sex god, or I was just insanely attracted to him.

My nails dug into his powerful arms as I held on to him, rocking with him as I felt the intense heat circulating through my veins and heading for the area right between my legs. Our lips touched, and I breathed into his mouth, just as we did during sex. Except we weren't having sex at all.

The sensation hit me hard, making me cry out and dig my nails harder into his skin. My heart skipped a beat because it couldn't keep up with the blood that I needed. I arched my back and grinded into him harder. "Oh god…"

Ryker pumped harder, pressing me against the couch as he panted.

My orgasm still lingered after it passed, like smoke hanging in the air from an old cigar. My pussy clenched around nothing, expecting his cock to be there.

Ryker suddenly pressed his lips to mine and gave a final grunt, his thrusts slowing down as he breathed harshly into my mouth. His cock hardened even further then suddenly began to soften.

He pulled away and looked into my eyes, satisfied and sex crazed at the same time. "Jesus, I just came in my boxers…"

I came in my underwear, and my panties were

soaked with my own fluid. "Brings back happy memories, huh?"

He stayed on top of me even though he was probably uncomfortable. "I wouldn't consider those moments to be good ones. But this...this is something I'll never forget." He kissed me before he pulled himself off me.

I continued to lay there because I was exhausted and satisfied. I wanted that strong body to return to mine again, to cuddle beside me as we fell asleep together. "I feel dirty."

He smiled before he walked away. "Then my job is done."

Vanessa knocked on my open door. "Dude, some super hot guy is here to see you."

"Super hot guy?" I skimmed through my calendar. "Do I have a meeting today?"

"No. He wanted to know if you're free for lunch."

It was probably Nathan. "Did you get his name?"

"I think it was Ryder... He was so hot, I couldn't really pay attention."

Then it was Ryker. He'd never stopped by my office and invited me to lunch before. After last night, my head was still in the clouds. His kiss, his body, his touch... everything was magical. "Oh..."

"You know this guy?"

"I'm kinda talking to him…"

"What?" She placed both of her hands on her hips. "A different hot guy took you to lunch last week. Now you have another boo? Girl, what's your secret?"

"Neither one of them are my boo. I'm just talking to them."

"You still need to teach me a thing or two."

Before I left, I made sure I changed into my heels. I didn't want to repeat the embarrassing episode I had with Nathan. I walked into the lobby and spotted Ryker sitting in the armchair, looking gloriously handsome in his fitted t-shirt and dark jeans. One of his legs was crossed, his ankle resting on the opposite knee. He shaved that morning, so his mouth was clean and smooth.

I wanted to stare at him a little longer before he noticed me.

I walked up to him, and the tap of my heels against the floor announced my presence. "You wanna take me to lunch?"

He looked me up and down, and when he reached my eyes, he winked. "I'd take a sexy lady like you out for lunch anytime."

Would I be a loser if I said that wink actually gave me chills? "That's cheesy, but I'm never gonna turn down a free meal."

He grinned. "That just makes you sexier." He stood up, rising to his full height on his long legs. "What are you in the mood for?"

"Anything."

"I like how simple you are." His arm moved around my waist effortlessly, and he guided me outside. He looked down at me as he led me down the sidewalk. "I like that dress."

It was one of my office dresses, simple and professional. I tried to stick to clothes that weren't too distracting, making people remember me for inappropriate reasons. Some women wore dresses that were too short for the office, or the kind that showed too much cleavage. I wanted to be remembered for my work, not my body. "Thanks."

"You look like a boss lady."

"I'm definitely not a boss. I just work in the marketing department."

"You're the director of the marketing department. Pretty big deal."

I shrugged it off, choosing to stay humble. "It's not like I'm retired in my thirties."

"Well, I didn't really work for that. I was given a lot of money, and I just invested it wisely."

"At least you didn't piss it away like most people."

He shrugged then guided me down the street. "How about Chinese? I could go for some chow mein."

"How about a poo-poo platter?" It was a stupid joke, and I regretted saying it the moment it came out of my mouth.

He stared down at me with a suppressed smile on his face. "You're cute, you know that?"

"It was a bad joke, and we both know it."

"Exactly. That's why it makes you cute." He pulled me into his side and pressed a kiss on my forehead. "And just for that, I'm gonna get the poo-poo platter. I've never tried it before."

"I haven't either. Wanna split one?"

"Sounds like a great idea."

———

We finished our meal, the empty plate between us demolished because we both liked it so much.

"What are you doing for the rest of the day?" I loved the way he filled out his t-shirts so perfectly. His chiseled physique was obvious even when he was dressed. His arms looked toned and big at the same time, muscular and lean.

"Playing video games."

"That's it?"

"Yep. I went to the gym in the morning, so I'm done for the day."

I wished that was my lifestyle, minus the gym part.

"Maybe I'll get into video games. See what the fuss is about."

"Greatest invention ever, other than sex."

"You can't invent sex. That's always been around."

"But not good sex." He winked.

The waiter brought our tab as well as two fortune cookies. Ryker quickly handed him the cash so I wouldn't have the opportunity to do the check dance. Ryker never let me pay for anything. He was far too stubborn for that.

"You know, you need to let me pay sometime."

"Nope."

"We live in a world where women are equals now."

"We'll never be equals."

My eyes narrowed on his face, my fire burning white-hot with rage. I was a bit of a feminist. I hated hearing both men and women make comments like that. It was bullshit.

He smiled when he saw my anger. "Women will always be superior. You're far more beautiful than us. Much smarter. More logical and compassionate. You'll always be the better sex, which is why men need to worship the ground you walk on."

My rage died quicker than a snap of a finger. I should have known Ryker didn't have any sexist views like other pigs I'd met in my lifetime. And I should have known he would say something sweet like that.

"I like getting a rise out of you." The smile never left his lips. "It's fun."

"You mean, you like making me mad."

"No. I just like getting you worked up. Your cheeks get red, and you look so cute."

"I do not look cute when I'm mad."

"I beg to differ." He handed me a fortune cookie and opened his own. He cracked the cookie then took the advice strip from the inside. "What does yours say?"

I unrolled mine. "Listen to your heart. It'll show you the way." It was vague but sweet. "What does yours say?"

He unrolled his then his eyes moved across the words. "The one you've been waiting for will walk into your life. Lock the door and never let them leave." He folded the paper in half then looked at me, a half smile on his face.

I wasn't sure if he made that up or if that's what it really said. I didn't dare ask since the air was tense between us. I broke off a piece of my cookie and ate it just so I had something to do.

He stuffed the fortune into his front pocket. "Need to get back to work?"

"Yeah, probably."

"Could I pay you to play with me all day?"

"That sounds like the best job in the world," I blurted. "But I do like my career."

"As much as getting laid for a living?" He waggled his eyebrows.

"Kinda sounds like I'd be a prostitute."

"But you'd be a classy prostitute."

I raised my eyebrows. "I don't think such a thing exists."

"You can start a trend." He rose from the table then extended his hand. "Think about it."

I took his hand, and we left the restaurant. We never walked anywhere with our hands held together like this. It made it seem like we were a couple, and the idea didn't scare me. Ryker was the first guy I'd dated that I pictured myself with in a serious manner. If only Ryker and I had solidified things before Nathan apologized to me, my life may have been more simple. I wouldn't have to choose between two guys because there would have only been one guy.

Ryker walked me back to the office, turning heads of the women that we passed. If he was aware of the constant stares, he didn't show it. For a man so unbelievably attractive, he was a lot humbler than anyone would expect.

"You don't have to walk me all the way inside."

"I don't mind." He opened the door for me, and we walked in together. "Besides, I gotta make sure all your coworkers know you're unavailable."

I wasn't committed to anyone, but I certainly was off

the market. "None of my coworkers are interested in me in that way."

He released a sarcastic snort. "Sure, sweetheart."

"I'm serious. Just because you find me attractive doesn't mean everyone else does."

"Trust me, every straight man in that office has checked you out. And all the lesbians too."

I swatted his arm playfully. "I'm kind of the office goof. I'm clumsy and make a lot of mistakes. People find it endearing, thankfully."

"Everything you do is cute, so I believe you." He stopped when we reached the lobby and didn't try to intrude by entering the hallway where my office was located. "I guess this is where I'll leave you."

"Okay." I faced him, feeling the same butterflies in my stomach as always. I had a great time with him. There was never a time when we hung out that we weren't laughing or being happy. It was like hanging out with Madeline...if she was a hot dude. "I'll see you later."

He cupped my face and craned his neck down to kiss me. It was office appropriate but a little long. His tongue stayed in his mouth, but his kiss was just as tantalizing without it. When he pulled away, he had that intense look in his eyes that said he didn't want the kiss to end. "How about tonight?"

I didn't have any plans, but I felt like Ryker was hogging most of my time. "I'm free."

E. L. TODD

"Great. Let's play laser tag."

I expected him to ask me out on a date—a romantic date. "What?"

"You've never played?"

"Not since I was ten…"

"I'll get everyone together. It'll be fun." He gave me a quick kiss on the lips before he walked away. "I'll pick you up at six."

134

8

RYKER

When I called Rae, Rex answered. "What's the scoop?"

"Rae, when did you start sounding like a dude?"

"It's me, dumbass," he said without identifying himself. "I stole Rae's phone to make her mad. Now that we don't live together, I'm running out of ways to tick her off. This is the only trick I have up my sleeve."

"Rex, give me the phone," Rae said in the background. "Zeke, grab it."

"I'm staying out of this," Zeke said.

"Rex!" Rae shouted.

"Anyway," Rex said. "How's the girl trouble?"

"It's getting better," I answered. "I think it is, at least."

"Have you tried the slippery dolphin?" Rex deadpanned.

"Oh my god." Rae finally got the phone back and put it to her ear. "Sorry about that. Everyone came over to watch the game."

"It's okay." Honestly, it was nice to talk to Rex as a friend again. "I didn't think he was ever going to stop hating me."

"At least put it on speaker phone," Rex said. "I want to know the dirt about this hot…I mean…mediocre chick that's just alright."

Rae put it on speaker phone. "Can you hear us, Ryker?"

"Loud and clear," I answered.

"Yo," Zeke said. "Zeke here."

Safari barked.

"What's up, guys?" I said. "I was just calling Rae for some chick advice."

"How's that going?" Rae asked.

"Pretty good. I invited her over for pizza, and we watched *Dumb and Dumber*."

"Best movie ever," Rex said.

"I surprised her at her office and took her to lunch," I continued. "We had a good time there. And then I invited her to play laser tag with a group of friends tonight."

"Damn," Rex said. "I want to date you. That sounds like fun."

"Thanks," I said with a chuckle. "I have no idea what the other guy is doing, so hopefully this is enough."

"The other guy is a douchebag," Rex said. "So he's probably doing douchebag things."

"You could always ask her," Rae said. "Feel her out on how she feels."

"That's too awkward," Zeke said. "That'll just make her uncomfortable. Act like you don't care. Be confident. Women respond to confidence. If you act like you're worried about Nathan, it's a turn off."

"That's true," Rex said in agreement. "Yeah, don't ask."

"What about one of her girlfriends?" Rae asked. "There's gotta be someone who's not a fan of Nathan."

"Well, her best friend isn't." Madeline and Liam both said the same thing to me.

"Perfect," Rae said. "Get the dirt from her since she's on your side."

"That feels deceitful," I said.

"Who cares?" Rex asked. "All is fair in love and war, right?"

"I think you should ask her," Rae said. "I doubt she's gonna tell Austen you're snooping around if you're the guy she wants Austen to be with."

"True," Zeke said.

I'd never put so much work into a single woman before, but here I was, trying to win over a woman I could have had a long time ago. I had three perfect months with her, and I should have sealed the deal then.

Before that dickface had the chance to grow some balls. "Yeah, maybe I will."

"Let us know what she says," Rae said. "We're all pretty invested now."

"Is this how people feel when they watch soap operas?" Rex asked. "And why are they called soap operas? Do they have anything to do with soap?"

"You're such an idiot," Rae said. "I swear, you get dumber and dumber."

"I'm the idiot?" Rex asked incredulously. "Weren't you the one that scored in the wrong hoop the other day?"

I suspected this fight would take a while.

"Ryker, we'll talk to you later," Zeke said. "Let us know how it goes." Just when Rae started to scream at Rex, Zeke hung up the phone.

"Thanks for meeting me." This time, I picked a random pizza parlor that Austen and I had never been to. I didn't want to run into her again like last time.

"No problem," Madeline said. "Austen told me that

she's got two guys on her leash now. That's a lot to juggle."

"I've only got one woman, and that's a lot to juggle."

"So, what did you want to talk about?" Her dark skin contrasted against the bright colors she wore. Anytime she wore yellow or blue, the vibrancy popped. It was perfect for a summer day. She had the same natural beauty that Austen possessed, but a different kind of elegance. I thought she was pretty, but I never felt any attraction. Come to think of it, it was very rare for me to be attracted to any woman besides Austen. There was Cheyenne, but that was forced. Even with Rae, I didn't want to jump her bones the way I used to.

"I need to know what she's saying about Nathan."

"You mean, the stuff she tells me?" She ordered a salad while I ordered two slices of pizza. As a dancer, I didn't expect her to eat something greasy and covered with cheese.

"Yeah."

"You want me to violate her confidence?"

"Not necessarily. I just want to know what Nathan is doing with her, what she likes and doesn't like. That way I can always be one step ahead."

She used her fork to mix her salad around. Her dressing was on the side but she never poured it into the bowl. It was probably too many calories even though she couldn't be any thinner without looking unhealthy. I was glad Austen had meat on her bones, curves on her frame. She complained about her belly and her ass, but damn, they were sexy. "I don't know…"

"Come on. You don't want her to end up with him, right?"

"Preferably, no. But I also don't want to interfere. I have to be supportive."

"You aren't interfering with her relationship with Nathan. You're just giving me some extra leverage. Big difference."

She stirred her salad around again before she finally took a bite. "I think she's gonna pick you. At least, I hope she does."

That gave me a rush of happiness I didn't expect. "Why do you think that?"

"You make her really happy. It's obvious every time I see her with you. Nathan is more of an…infatuation. But they don't have a friendship. They don't have fun the way you do. You know what I mean?"

I didn't have a clue. "Not really."

"I think she wants to be with Nathan for the wrong reasons. I think she used to be really happy and thinks she can get that back if they work it out. But she doesn't understand that you could make her way happier than he ever did if she just wasn't so scared. She wants to stick with what she knows rather than taking another risk."

"Maybe you should give up dancing and be a shrink instead."

She laughed. "No, thanks. No one likes a shrink."

Liam would like her no matter what.

"She needs to let Nathan go. He's given her the closure she needs to finally move on. But she's gotta figure that out on her own."

"But you think she prefers me?"

"I think she does...deep down inside."

That made me feel a little better. "I hope you're right."

"Even though Nathan cheated on her, he's hard to compete with. They were engaged, after all. So she sees him differently than anyone else."

"I wish she would focus on why they never got married."

"I don't know," she said. "Austen was really messed up for a long time. The only progress I ever saw her make was when you came around. I'm glad she's forgiven him so she can move on. But I wish she would move on rather than give him the time of day."

"Me too..."

"I'll let you know how things are going with him. She hasn't said much."

"Really?" I asked in disappointment.

"She's told me she thinks you're incredible and

perfect and she wishes she didn't have feelings for Nathan at all."

That was another hopeful sign.

"I think she was in love with you...could possibly still be in love with you."

My attention piqued even more at that part.

"But I think Nathan has made her forget that. Her feelings are so complicated that I can't understand them, so I doubt she understands them either."

Looks like it's going to be an uphill battle.

Madeline watched the disappointment stretch across my face. "Sorry, I know I wasn't much help. Next time she talks to me, I'll let you know what she says about her and Nathan."

"Thanks. I appreciate that."

"And just so you know, I'm rooting for you."

I nodded. "Thanks again."

"I don't think Nathan would hurt her again, but what he did was pretty terrible. Austen deserves to be with a guy that gets it right the first time. He doesn't need to screw up and lose her before he understands how valuable she is."

I did the same thing, but at a much lesser degree. I wouldn't make the same mistake twice. "Yeah…"

I crouched down behind a box and found Austen. My gun was cradled against my chest, lit up in the dark from the UV light. "Jared is in place on the other side of the room. We only got two minutes to win this thing."

"We've got em. Like shooting fish in a barrel." She held the gun on top of the box, her body crouched down and mostly hidden from sight.

"We're only up by a few hundred points. Gotta make sure they don't get us."

"If I'm going down, I'm taking everyone with me." She kept her eyes glued on the door, her finger on the trigger.

I lost focus when I stared at her in her laser tag vest and gun. She took the game way more seriously than I expected, and it was another cute quality I didn't expect to see. "You look so fucking cute right now."

"What?" She dropped her gaze from the target and looked at me.

I wish I could push her back to the floor and fuck her right in the middle of the course, but there were cameras everywhere. I spoke louder so she could hear me over the music. "You. Look. Cute."

Just then, Liam ran inside with Madeline and Jenn. Jared started to fire off but only got in a few shots before all three turned on him.

"This is it, sweetheart." I used the box to hold my gun as I kneeled and fired. I hit Jenn in the back because she was the easiest target. Liam kept moving and Madeline crouched to the floor. "Just keep firing." We had less than sixty seconds left, so we needed to get as many points as possible.

Liam was the first one to figure out where we were hiding. When he noticed his vest kept lighting up but Jared was hidden behind the wall, he knew he wasn't alone. He turned around, spotted us, and then sprinted toward us.

"Shit, he's coming!" Austen said.

"Don't stop shooting."

Liam aimed his gun and began to fire back before he dodged behind a pillar. Before he could take any more shots at us, the timer went off and the lights turned on. All weapons were suspended, and the game ended.

"You guys are such cheaters." Liam dropped his gun with attitude. "You totally ambushed us."

"That's how we roll," Austen said. "It's not our fault you didn't come in here with a game plan."

"You heard my woman." I wrapped my arm around her shoulder and walked her out. "Step it up."

Liam rolled his eyes then grabbed Madeline. "We'll get them back another time."

I moved my lips to Austen's ear. "Yeah right."

Liam kept walking and didn't turn around. "I heard that."

"Said it pretty loud," I teased.

Jared walked to our side. "We kicked their asses. Pathetic." He high-fived Austen then did the same to me.

"It's from playing all those video games," Austen said. "It's starting to really pay off."

"Yep," I said. "Just like I knew it would." We returned our equipment then walked out of the building. "You guys wanna get some grub?"

Liam was still in a sour mood, but he tried to hide it. "Sure. You wanna go to Riot? I could use a beer."

"Me too," Austen said. "In a frosty mug with fries."

I pulled her tighter into my side. "You're the perfect woman. You know that?"

Austen smiled then quickly looked away like she was trying to hide her natural reaction. "If all I need to do is drink beer and eat fries, then your standards are pretty low."

"You'd be surprised. Not too many women like beer."

"But we all love fries," she said. "So every woman in America fits half your criteria. My mom loves beer more than anyone else I know. Maybe she's your soul mate."

I grinned. "She is pretty hot…"

"Gross!" She smacked my arm as we walked on the sidewalk. "That's my mom."

"So what? That's exactly where you get your good looks from. It all makes sense."

"Hey." Liam turned around and walked backwards. "I don't care if you tease Austen, but her mom is my mom.

And you need to stop checking out my mother because that's a violation of the bro code."

"Violation?" Jared asked. "He's already banging your sister."

Liam cringed before he turned around and grabbed Madeline's hand again.

"Does that mean my dad is hot too?" she asked.

"Yeah, he's not bad," I said. "But I've always shopped in the chick department."

We arrived at the bar then got a booth in the corner, the perfect place to see the big TVs in every corner of the room. We ordered a round of beers and plates of fries so Austen would be happy. We got one of every flavor since she couldn't make up her mind.

"Sweet potato, garlic, cheese, and regular," Jared said. "That's a lot of fries."

"They're all delicious in their own ways," Austen said as she grabbed a handful of each and dropped them onto her plate.

I stole one and popped it into my mouth.

She gave me the death look.

"What?" I asked. "I just had your back in the middle of a war zone. You won't share some fries with me?"

"You could order your own, you know."

I looked at the four basket of fries, which was enough to feed the entire table. "No way in hell you're gonna eat all this by yourself."

"You don't know Austen very well then," Jared said. "She won the country pie eating contest a few years ago."

Austen puffed up her chest like she was proud. "First in the young women's division, thank you very much."

Jesus Christ, could she get any cuter? "Did you get a trophy?"

"A ribbon. It's still on my fridge."

How did I miss that? "Wow. Your finest accomplishment."

"It is my finest accomplishment," she said proudly. "Everyone said I couldn't do it. Well, I proved them wrong."

"But she packed on ten pounds for it," Liam jabbed.

"Whatever," Austen said. "It was totally worth it."

"You look perfect the way you are, so those pounds just made you look sexier." My arm moved around her shoulder, and my fingers felt some of her hair. It was smooth for now, but in a few hours, I would tangle it up with my fist.

"Well, I dropped the weight shortly afterward," Austen said. "Stopped eating for a month."

"Looks like you need to enter that contest again," I said. "I'll be in the audience cheering you on."

"God no." She rolled her eyes at the memory. "I felt so sick at the end. I threw up at least three pies in the porta-potty."

"But you could add another ribbon to the fridge," I reminded her.

"One is plenty," she said. "One day, I'll hang it up next to my MIT degree."

"I say you take your degree down altogether," Jared said. "Doesn't mean shit compared to that ribbon."

"I have to agree with Jared on that one," I said. "No comparison."

She rolled her eyes and dumped her fries into her ketchup one by one.

"You put cheesy fries into ketchup?" I asked in disgust.

She was drinking her beer when she heard my question. She gulped it down then turned to me. "Why are you always picking on me?"

"Because you're cute," I said. "But in this case, you're just weird. I've never seen anyone do that."

"First time for everything, right?" she said.

I grabbed one of her cheese fries and dipped it into the ketchup before I popped it into my mouth. I tried to get over the taste but I couldn't. Cheese and ketchup didn't mix. "This is gross. I'm sorry, sweetheart."

"What?" she asked incredulously. "You know what people put on cheeseburgers? Ketchup."

"But this cheese is different," I argued. "It's nacho cheese."

"Whatever," she said as she ate another one. "Cheese is cheese."

"Girl, not all cheeses are created equal," Madeline said. "We all know that."

"Why don't you pick on Liam, Madeline, and Jenn?" she asked as she grabbed the handle to her mug. "They just lost, remember?"

I grinned while I watched her slurp down her beer like a man. "It's more fun to pick on you. You get all mad. And when you're mad, you look even cuter. It's something about the way your eyes change."

She set her mug down with attitude, making it clank against the table. "Wait until I pick on you for something."

"Like what?" I asked.

"You know…" She searched everyone's expression as she tried to come up with something. Her fingers spun a sweet potato fry as she fidgeted at the table.

"Like what?" I repeated. "What could you possibly pick on me for?" I was boring and uninteresting. I didn't have cute quirks or unusual preferences. I slept in every day, hit the gym, and then played video games all day long. I wasn't smart or a hard worker like she was. Maybe she was a nerd, but that was definitely a compliment. She was a strong and successful woman who conquered a male dominated field. She wasn't just interesting, but inspiring.

"Uh…I'll think of something." She placed the fry in her mouth. "Just give me some time."

"Whatever you say, sweetheart." My arm draped over the back of the chair, and I leaned in to press a kiss on her cheek.

She stilled at the affection, probably because she never felt my lips on her cheek like that.

"Aww," Madeline whispered under her breath.

Austen tried to pretend she didn't hear what her friend said by looking down at her fries. She put a few into her mouth, ignoring the heavy silence that began to grow. Jared tried to break the ice by changing the subject. "Anyone wanna order some hot wings?"

"My place or yours?" I asked as we walked together up the street.

"I should probably head home. I've got to wake up early in the morning."

"Then your place, it is." We were already going in that direction, so we didn't need to change our route.

"Well…I thought we weren't sleeping together?" Her small hand felt perfect in mine, warm and soft.

"But we can go to sleep together, right?" There was no harm in that, even if we were naked together under the sheets. We could control ourselves, right? "Unless you need some space." I'd been hogging her for nearly three days in a row. I'm sure Nathan wasn't too pleased about that. But the more time she spent me with me, the less time she spent with him.

"No, not at all," she said quickly, her hand squeezing mine. "I just…when you're naked, I have a hard time behaving myself."

Then maybe she shouldn't behave herself. "I'll be a gentleman, I promise. I miss sleeping with you. It's like taking Nyquil. It knocks me out."

"So I'm a narcotic?" she asked with a laugh.

"But in a good way."

"How can that be in a good way?"

"As in, you give me the best sleep I've ever gotten." We walked together and entered her building. She was on the second story so she was close to the sidewalk and the foot traffic. Sometimes I heard sirens go off in the middle of the night and honking from annoyed drivers, but I'd still rather sleep with her than alone. If I went to my penthouse across town, it would be quiet and sleek. But it would be lonely too.

We got undressed then slipped inside her bed. She wore one of her old college t-shirts and just her panties, looking like a wet dream. I kept my boxers on even though the thin fabric would do nothing to protect her from my raging hard on. Like a switch, he turned on the second she walked into the room.

She had a queen size bed, smaller than the king I had at home. It was old and hard, but that didn't stop me from getting comfortable. Her alarm would go off at the crack of dawn and wake me up, and she would hit the snooze button five times before she finally got out of bed. But that was still preferable than being without her.

I pulled her against me, her leg hooked over my waist and my hard dick pressed into her stomach. While I was throbbing, I didn't put the moves on her. I wanted to be more than just a great lay to her. I wanted to be the man she wanted to go to sleep with, not just screw. We had a special connection, a chemistry that ignited even when we didn't touch, but we also had a profound friendship. I could feel it in the trust we had for one another. She could tell me anything, and I could confess my darkest secrets to her.

That kind of beauty was rare.

The lights from the street filtered through her blinds and brought an unwanted glow into the apartment, but it allowed me to stare at her when all the lights were off. I could see the beautiful curve of her lips, the narrow point of her nose, and even her thick eyelashes. Nothing could keep my interest indefinitely, not even video games, but this woman stole my fascination the first time I looked at her. It'd been months, and I still didn't want to look away, to miss just a second of her beautiful face. I wouldn't change anything about her, loving all her quirkiness and uniqueness. She was definitely one of a kind.

Her hand moved up my bare chest, and she stared at her fingertips resting against my skin. Her eyelashes moved every time she blinked. The movement was slow since her eyes were lidded and heavy. It was obvious she was tired, fighting to keep her eyes open. "Ryker?"

"Yes, sweetheart?" I wanted time to stand still, to make this moment last forever. It was just her and me against the world. There was no Nathan. There was no Rae. It was just the two of us.

"Did that fortune cookie really say that?"

Since I didn't expect her to ask that question, not in a million years, I wasn't prepared to hear it. "Say what?"

"About that person walking into your life?"

I knew exactly what she was referring to, but I kept the same stoic expression. My fingers moved up and into her hair, feeling the soft strands I loved to tangle around my fingertips. My cock slowly softened as my thoughts diminished my arousal. She asked a question I wanted to dodge, but I didn't know how to accomplish that.

Since she was tired, I tried to lull her to sleep with my touch. I continued to touch her, to drag my hands down the back of her neck and across her shoulders. When she blinked, her eyes remained closed longer every single time.

I listened to her breath as it grew quiet and steady. She was slowly drifting away, falling asleep without waiting for my answer.

Finally, her eyes closed and didn't open again. But her lips moved. "You aren't going to answer me, are you?"

My fingers stilled in the center of her back, feeling the warm and smooth skin against my fingertips. Her chest rose and fell at a steady rate. I could feel her back expand with every breath she took. She suddenly felt fragile to me, vulnerable and easily breakable. I wanted to devote my life to her protection, to guard her heart so it would never be broken again. I didn't want Nathan to win because he didn't deserve her. He already hurt her once, and he shouldn't get a second chance.

And I shouldn't get a second chance with Rae either.

But I would be different with Austen. I would always be faithful and honest, and I certainly wouldn't repeat the same mistake I made in the past. Hearing those three little words from Rae sent me on a rampage that took months to recover from. By the time it was over, it was too late.

Hopefully, it wasn't too late for Austen. "You already know the answer."

9

AUSTEN

After spending the last few days with Ryker, my heart was smitten all over again. He always made me smile, and he was so handsome, it should be illegal. He was a human teddy bear who kept me warm all night and even the innocent way he touched me sent chills down my spine.

Nathan slowly faded from my mind.

I started to weigh the two men against each other, and after spending time with Ryker, Nathan's past transgressions seemed to work harder against him than they did before. I tried to remember the last time he made me laugh, and I couldn't recall the most recent instance. Ryker's rugged jawline entered my mind throughout the day, and I pictured how those soft lips felt against my own.

Could I really walk away from him?

He was my best friend.

I was walking on my treadmill desk when Vanessa poked her head in my office. "Hot guy #1 is here."

I hit the stop button and glanced at the time. The workday was over and people were already gone. I only stayed behind because I was adding the finishing touches on my final campaigns. "Hot guy #1?"

"Yeah." She waggled her eyebrows. "The buff guy with dirty blond hair."

Nathan. "Thanks for letting me know." I shut my laptop and stepped off the platform.

Vanessa kept staring at me.

"What?"

"Nothing. My life is just so much more boring than yours." She flipped her hair over her shoulder and walked off.

I changed my shoes this time then walked into the lobby with my purse over my shoulder. My stomach tightened in knots like it usually did when I was anywhere near Nathan, but this time, the sensation was different. I wasn't as excited as I usually was, probably because Ryker had thickened my mind with a heavy fog.

I turned the corner and saw him standing with his hands in his pockets. He wore black jeans and a dark green t-shirt, showing off his muscular arms and chest. He had long and toned legs, the kind that were muscular but not overly buff. He had thin hips that made his jeans hang down perfectly. And his butt looked great in the back, I was certain of it.

My temperature increased by a few degrees.

I'd forgotten how hot he was.

Like, scorching hot.

My throat suddenly went dry, and I swallowed to moisten my mouth. I walked up to him feeling a little less confident and a little more self-conscious. "What a nice surprise."

"Wanted to take you to dinner, if you're free."

Ryker hadn't asked me to do anything yet, but I was certain that was bound to happen in the next hour. Nathan beat him to the punch. "I'm free, and I could eat. But you know me, I can always eat."

The corner of his mouth raised in a slight smile. "Like I could forget." His large hand slid around my back and rested on the steep curve just above my butt. He leaned down and pressed a kiss to my lips, his slight beard rubbing against my skin.

Now my head was in the clouds again.

Nathan was a great kisser. He knew how to make a gentle and innocent kiss so much more. He didn't need to use his tongue to expression his passion. His hand tightened on the back of my dress, bunching up the fabric and making it rise up my legs.

My hands rested against his chest, and I automatically rose on my tiptoes as he pulled me closer into him. I felt the spark, that chemistry that burned me from the inside out. Sex with Nathan used to be great. I still remembered the last time we made love and how good it was. None of the guys I met after we broke up compared—until I met Ryker.

Nathan broke away first, which was a good thing because I was pretty paralyzed. His hand slid from my back, and he grabbed my hand. "Let's go before I get carried away."

***

Nathan took me to a fancy Italian place I'd never heard of, and we enjoyed a bottle of wine and way too much food. When I sat across from him, I always felt nervous even though I shouldn't. As a result, I didn't eat as much as I normally would, and I certainly fidgeted a lot more. The muscles of my stomach were tight because the nerves were getting to me. I wish I could be cool with Nathan, but I just couldn't.

When it came to Ryker, I was totally relaxed.

I wasn't sure what the difference between the two men was. One gave me butterflies in my stomach, and the other made me laugh so hard water came out of my nose.

When dinner was over, Nathan took my hand and guided me back to his place.

"There's something I want to show you."

"What is it?" We used to hold hands all the time, and I noticed how natural it felt. Like no time had passed at all, our bodies fit together perfectly. We used to do this exact same thing when we took walks around the park or the mall. Only then, I was wearing a diamond ring on my finger.

I never had the strength to throw it away. Nathan never asked for it back, and I couldn't pawn it for cash. I shoved it into a box inside my nightstand, where it remained untouched for years.

"You'll see." He took me to his building, which wasn't too far from mine. We were only a few blocks apart, much closer together than I was to Ryker's place. He was on the fourth floor, but he took the elevator to the very top.

This was getting interesting.

My phone vibrated with a text message, and I quickly pulled it out to check the screen.

Wanna eat pizza naked in my hot tub? Ryker's name appeared on the screen.

The idea was actually very tempting. But I was already with Nathan, and I couldn't just leave now, not when he took me to a nice dinner and we were having a great time. I didn't want to tell Ryker what I was really doing because it was awkward so I wrote something vague. *I have a plans tonight. But maybe tomorrow.*

Ryker would know exactly what I was doing. *Tomorrow, then.* The dots disappeared.

I dropped my phone back into my purse and hoped Nathan didn't take a peek at the screen. The elevator doors opened, and we walked to the stairs that led to the very top of the roof.

"Now I'm really interested to see what we're doing."

"You'll love it. Trust me." He guided me to the roof where two lounge chairs sat with an ice chest and a portable fire pit. Marshmallow sticks sat on the table, along with all the ingredients to make s'mores.

"Wow…"

"I wanted to take you camping, but I knew that would be too difficult in Manhattan. So I brought camping to us."

"Minus the bears and raccoons," I said with a chuckle.

He got the fire going then pulled out two bottles of beer from the ice chest. "The lights are too bright to see the stars. But we can still enjoy the view."

I took a seat and watched him twist off the cap to my beer. He handed it over then sat beside me, his chair close enough that our hands could touch as they sat on the armrests. He took a drink and gazed across the city to the lit skyscrapers surrounding us.

I could hear the sound of sirens in the distance, the hum of traffic far down below as the stoplights turned green and the cars sped up again. The city was always loud, but that turned into background noise once I got used to it. Silence was unheard of in the city that never slept. If I were alone in the wilderness, I'd probably be terrified of the silence. Being in close proximity to people, even some of the terrifying people of New York, was preferable to being alone. "And it is a lovely view."

He stuck marshmallows on the ends of our sticks then handed one to me. "You like yours brown or burned?"

"Brown." I held my stick over the fire, doing my best to make sure the marshmallow didn't get caught in the flames. "But I'm too impatient and always try to rush it, so it burns to a crisp."

He made a disgusted face. "I hate burned marshmallows." He held his stick higher than mine, in no rush to get it browned. "I'll take my sweet ass time to avoid it."

"But when the marshmallow gets too hot, it'll start to melt and drip off."

He eyed me from his chair, a smile on his lips. "Not your first rodeo, huh?"

"My dad used to take Liam and me camping when he

161

first adopted me." I didn't talk about my early childhood much. I remembered the foster home vaguely, and the day my parents walked in and filled out the paperwork to take me home. They loved me right from the start, and my dad included me in all activities. He taught me how to set up a tent, start a fire, survive in the wilderness, and fish. He was never prejudiced against me because I was a girl—something I appreciated.

Nathan nodded, probably because he didn't know how else to respond to my comment. He knew I struggled with my adoption, knowing my own father didn't want me after my mother ran off. He knew my deepest fears—all of them.

So he knew exactly how much it hurt when he left.

The thought filled me with pain that I thought I'd parted with. I forgave Nathan because he seemed sincere, but no amount of forgiveness could ever erase the pain. He knew I was strong and courageous, but he also knew I had one particular weakness.

Feeling abandoned.

Nathan cleared his throat and turned over his marshmallow. "Yours is starting to brown."

I turned it over and spotted the brown coloring on top. It was starting to form a hard shell with a gooey center. Once I was finished and it was smeared on a graham cracker, it would be delicious. "It's looking pretty good." I eyed his as it was held higher above the fire. "Yours looks exactly the same. Bring it a little lower."

"I don't know…"

"Come on, it'll be fine."

He brought his marshmallow to my level and rotated it so all the sides were exposed.

"Don't turn the stick. Let it sit so it has a chance to brown. If you keep spinning it, it'll just melt and drop into the fire."

"Good point. Forgot you were an eagle scout."

"Damn right."

We watched the flames and kept our eyes glued to our marshmallows. It was a little like fishing, but without bait at the end. My marshmallow turned a perfect brown color, and I pulled it away from the fire. "This is the nicest marshmallow I've ever seen." I felt the surface with my fingers, noticing the crust.

"That does look good." Nathan threw together graham crackers and a piece of chocolate and held it out to me so I could wipe the marshmallow across the chocolate. Immediately, the chocolate began to sweat from the heat. He placed the other graham cracker on top then handed it over. "Congratulations."

"Why, thank you." I handed his stick back.

He examined his marshmallow then returned it to the fire. "Mine needs a few more minutes."

When I took a bite, I got chocolate and marshmallow

on my face, but I didn't bother wiping it off. It was a waste of time. May as well wait until the feast was over.

Nathan grinned as he watched me.

"What?"

His smile grew. "Nothing."

"It's so not nothing." I finished the last bite then sucked my fingers. "What?"

"You're messy, that's all."

"I'd like to see you try to eat this and not get it everywhere."

He chuckled. "Challenge accepted." He pulled his marshmallow out and got his s'more ready. He gave me a cocky expression but he placed the whole thing in his mouth and chewed it with his mouth closed. "See?"

"That doesn't count."

He kept chewing and shrugged.

"You aren't supposed to shove a whole piece of food in your mouth like that. That's how people choke and die."

He kept chewing until he finally got the whole thing broken down. "Whatever. I didn't make a mess."

"You and your big mouth…"

He laughed then pressed another marshmallow onto the edge of his stick. "You're just jealous that I'm smarter than you."

"I don't want to scarf the whole thing in one bite. I want to take my time."

"And make a mess." He pointed to my hair on the left side of my face. "You got it in your hair, by the way."

"I did?" I felt the strand with my fingers and noted the stickiness. I tried to clean it but it seemed like I was just making it worse. The texture stuck between my fingers, and every time I broke them apart, I seemed to spread it further and further.

Nathan chuckled at my inadequacy then grabbed a paper towel and wetted it. "Try this." He handed it over.

I scraped the chunks from my hair then took care of my fingertips. "Thanks."

"You want another one?" He grabbed my stick and nodded to the bag of marshmallows.

"I'm gonna cut myself off. Clearly, I can't handle those things."

"If you shoved the whole thing in your mouth, you could."

I suddenly pictured shoving something else in my mouth, something I used to do for him first thing in the morning. I hadn't been with Nathan in years, but I never forgot his size and length. I stared at the fire and tried to think of something else.

Nathan put his stick aside, clearly done with the marshmallows. "You like it up here?"

"I do." I surveyed the lights of the city, appreciating them like stars in the heavens.

"Do you want to stay in the city for the rest of your life?"

"I don't know." I had a great job and a decent apartment in the greatest city of the world. I wasn't sure if I could feel at home anywhere else. "I mean, it would be nice to get some peace and quiet once in a while, but other than that, I like it here. Maybe one day I'll buy a house like my parents. It's not exactly the suburbs, but it's not an apartment either."

He adjusted his position in the chair and straightened his t-shirt. "You aren't interested in Connecticut then?"

The only reason why I wanted to live there was to raise a family. I'd been single for a long time, so that dream of growing my family only became more and more distant. Now I didn't even think about it anymore. "Not really. Suburbs wouldn't suit me well."

Nathan didn't ask me more questions about it. Hopefully, he realized I only wanted to move from the city because we needed a house with a yard for our dog and two kids. But men were pretty dense sometimes.

"What about you? Are you happy in the city that never sleeps?"

He shrugged. "Sometimes I like the cacophony, the fact there's always something going on. I can get Chinese food at three in the morning or pick up groceries in the middle of the night. But other times, I want space. I want to look out my front window and not see a person for miles around. I want to open my window and only hear the sound of the wind. I know I'll always have to work in the city, but I wouldn't mind commuting if I got to have a piece of that—like a compromise."

"Then why don't you move?"

He shrugged. "I don't want to buy a house until I settle down. I want to pick out the place with her, make sure we both have exactly what we want." He turned his gaze on me, watching me with a look that was full of intensity. He didn't say anything else, but his meaning was clear on the surface.

I couldn't hold the look, so I turned away, feeling the tension fall on my shoulders. If he had it his way, we'd be back together and choosing that house right that moment. It was sweet, but it was also suffocating. We would have already had all of that if he hadn't betrayed me. He was the only one to blame for his unhappiness.

He was the only one to blame for my unhappiness.

Nathan looked away and rubbed the scruff along his chin. He didn't have the audacity to say anything more, to pressure me about the dreams we used to have.

I remembered the way my whole world went up in flames. My mom had just spent ten thousand dollars on a dress I never got to wear. I came home with it protected in plastic and spotted Nathan fucking Lily on my bed.

Could I ever really let that go?

Could I ever really wipe that memory away?

Nathan must have read my mind because he said, "I'm sorry. I know you've already forgiven me, but I'll say it as many times as it takes. I don't want you to forget how terrible I feel, how much I wish I could take everything back and go back to where we were."

I believed the sincerity of his words, but I also couldn't forget the pain that burned in my heart.

He walked me to my door with his head slightly bowed. When I pulled out my keys from my purse, he leaned against the doorway and watched me. "I'm sorry, I shouldn't have said all of that about Connecticut. It was stupid."

"You don't need to apologize. You didn't mean anything vicious by it."

"But I saw the look in your eyes. Thinking about the house we never bought and the life we never lived hurt you. It's been years, and I still hurt you. The more I think about what I did and how I handled the situation, the more I hate myself for my stupidity. I'm trying to get you back because I love you, but I think the right thing to do is let you go. But I don't want to do that…because I'm selfish."

I crossed my arms over my chest, at a loss of what to say. "Honestly, I wish I could just get over you and move on with my life. I'm not giving you a second chance because I want to or even think you deserve it…I just haven't stopped loving you."

He nodded slightly. "I'm damn lucky."

"Or I'm damn stupid."

"I don't think you're stupid," he said gently. "I would never hurt you again. I know that's hard to believe based on what I did, but I mean that. You don't have anything to worry about. If you really want to make this work, we'll live a long and happy life together. I'll be the most devoted guy on the planet. I'll never take you for granted because I know what it's like to lose you. If you love me and want to make this work, we will succeed."

All of that sounded nice in theory, but my heart had never really fixed itself from the initial heartbreak. I would judge any woman for going back to her cheating ex, and I certainly judged myself right now. But I loved those kisses, that handsome smile, and everything else about him.

What was wrong with me?

I got the door unlocked and dropped my keys back into my purse.

"Can I come inside?" he whispered.

My hand moved to the door but I didn't look up. If I invited him inside, there would be kissing and touching. Thinking about our past and possible future made me pull away, made me lift my guard. "Not tonight."

Nathan didn't press the invite, just like the gentleman he was. "Can we have dinner tomorrow?"

I didn't have any plans, and for some reason, I didn't want to reject him. "Sure."

A small smile appeared on his lips, a slight hint of hope. "I'll see you then." His arm moved around my waist and he pulled me into his chest for a hug. He didn't try to kiss me, reading my body language pretty well. But he held me there for a long time like he never wanted to let me go. His hard body felt like a mountain pressed against mine, and every time he took a deep breath, I could feel it push against me. His other arm locked around my waist until he had a firm grip around my body. His chin rested on top of my head and he moved slightly from side to side, like he was slow dancing with me.

When he held me this close, I forgot about all the pain between us. All I felt was the closeness, the goodness. He used to hold me like this all the time, and whenever he did, I knew everything would be okay.

Maybe everything would be okay.

10

RYKER

I texted Austen. *Let's get grub tonight—and eat naked.*

The three dots appeared, followed by her disappointing answer. *Already have plans. How about tomorrow?*

She was seeing him two nights in a row? What the hell? I saw her three days in a row, but I just assumed that meant she liked spending time with me. But it seemed like she liked spending time with him just as much.

Shit.

Tomorrow works. I had to keep my cool and pretend to be okay with this nightmare, but I was losing my grip on sanity. She had a thirty-day window to make her decision, and I was beginning to think I gave her too

E. L. TODD

much time. I had to just brush it off and pretend to be indifferent to the whole thing.

Which was fucking hard.

I'll see you then.

I read her last message with a jolt of pain then called Madeline.

"Hello, Ryker," she said with her definitively cool voice. "I figured you would be calling soon."

"What's the dirt?"

"It's both good and bad."

I wish I could just hear the good stuff and forget the bad stuff ever happened. "Hit me."

"Good stuff is, she said she forgives him but she still feels the pain. It comes back and haunts her all the time. She's not sure if she'll ever really get over it. The expensive wedding dress her mother bought her is still sitting in her closet. She bought it the day she came home and caught Nathan. She said she just can't forget those kinds of memories..."

I stared at my TV in the living room without paying attention to what was on. Once I heard Madeline tell me that, I felt like shit. It was one of the lowest sensations in the world, the kind of pain that felt heavy in the pit of my stomach. She had a special day with her mom picking out her wedding dress, something women dreamed about their entire lives, and Nathan was screwing Lily on their bed? It was so despicable I thought it couldn't be real.

"But then she says she still loves him…and can't let it go. So she doesn't know what to do. She likes spending time with him because they have fun and those feelings are still there, but she's afraid at the same time."

My patience was disappearing, and my anger was rising. I wanted Austen to pick me because she wanted me, but now I wanted to murder Nathan so he wasn't in the running at all. She wasn't my girl, but I looked at her like she was. And this fucking asshole hurt my girl.

"Ryker?"

"I'm still here…"

"You've been quiet for a while."

"I hate Nathan even more now. I can't believe he did that to her."

"I know. I can't believe it either. The wedding dress is still in her closet. I saw it the other week."

She probably felt bad getting rid of it because it cost so much money, but she could never wear it again, even if she did marry Nathan. It would only remind her of that terrible day when she found out the truth. "I can't let him win."

"I know."

"She deserves so much better than him. I'm not saying I'm perfect, but I would never pull something like that."

"I know that too," she said.

"They're hanging out tonight?"

"Getting dinner."

When I pictured her sitting across from him, it made me angry all over. I was grateful we agreed to no sex because that would make everything worse. If she was fucking him, I couldn't handle it. The thought of them kissing was already painful enough, but anything more than that would make me shoot my brains out.

"What's your plan?"

"I don't have one. I've just been myself so far, but maybe that isn't good enough."

"It is," she said firmly. "Let Austen run her course with Nathan. It's one of those things you just have to do. Let her see what it would be like with Nathan again. She'll realize it can never be anything like it was before, and she'll finally move on."

"Yeah, maybe."

"Don't worry about it, Ryker. I don't think anything could ever really happen."

"What makes you so sure?" I was wealthy and not bad to look at, but my skills didn't extend beyond that.

"She's pretty close with her parents. She has her complaints because she knows they love Liam more than her, but she hates disappointing them. They would never welcome Nathan back into their lives. They wouldn't necessarily be rude to him, but they would definitely tell her it was a mistake."

That's true. No parent would be cool with that. "You're right. That could be my saving grace."

"Not to mention, Liam would never be on board with it. Neither will Jared or Jenn. Like I said, let her get this out of her system. She's been heartbroken for the last three years trying to find herself. This will give her the closure that she needs."

I hated being patient like this because I was an impatient man, but I understood what Madeline was saying.

"She's lucky you're still fighting for her."

I didn't think twice before I blurted out the first thing that came to my mind. "We're supposed to be together. Of course I'm going to fight for her."

I prepped everything and began cooking when I knew she would arrive soon. From what I gathered from Madeline, Nathan never cooked for her. That was something I could beat him at. Nothing was more romantic for a woman than having a man cook for her. It was a nice change of roles.

She knocked on the door.

I felt a jolt of nerves run through my body,

something I didn't usually feel. It was rare for me to ever feel nervous around anyone for any reason, but Austen gave me a little dose of anxiety. Maybe it was because I was scared I was going to lose, or maybe it was because I was just excited to see her.

Whatever the case, I knew she was special to me.

I washed my hands before I answered the door. I plastered on a smile and tried to forget that Nathan existed at all. When she was in my apartment, there was nothing that existed outside of that door. It was just her and me—against the world.

I opened the door and looked down at the beautiful woman who captured my complete affection. With blue eyes that reminded me of the Virgin Islands and a smile that could light up the darkest sky, she was the most amazing thing in the world. "Hey."

Her features slowly changed, her joy growing until it reached every inch of her face. Sometimes I saw her smile at people when she met them, trying to be polite and make a good impression. But I could tell that smile was fake. I could tell it was just a front, a mask. But when she smiled at me like that, like how she was right then and there, I knew it was genuine. I knew she felt the same excitement deep inside her gut that I felt. "Hey."

My arms circled her waist and I pulled her into my chest, my mouth aching to kiss hers. I loved the shape of her body, the deep curve in her back that led to her petite torso. I loved the spot right underneath her shoulder blades. I cradled her into me and explored her mouth with mine. I didn't think about her kissing Nathan over the past few days. When we were together, it was just the two of us.

One hand migrated into her hair, and I felt the soft strands that slid past my fingertips. Smooth as silk and heavy with vanilla, her hair was a major turn on. I loved finding it on my pillow, my couch, and around my cock. Other people might complain about the strands sprinkled all over the apartment, but I adored them.

I backed her up into the door and kissed her harder, forgetting about the chicken on the stove. My hands gripped hers and I pinned them against the wood, our fingertips interlocked. I'd fucked her right against this door before, her legs wrapped around my waist. As much as I wanted to do that, I kept my cock in my pants —even though he was about to break through my zipper.

Our tongues moved together as we tasted each other, greeting each other in the most intimate way possible. Kissing was sexier than fucking sometimes. It was personal, invading. Long make out sessions weren't my thing, not since high school, but they were awesome with Austen.

But it made me want to fuck her too.

I pulled away and looked into her face, my chest rising and falling from my heavy breathing. I missed the way she used to come over and we got right down to business. I took our relationship for granted and knew how much I missed it now that it was gone.

I shouldn't have been such an idiot.

My hand finally released her hair, and I stepped away. "Hungry?"

"Definitely."

I suspected she was hungry for more than food, but since there wasn't a damn thing I could do about it, I held back my dirty comment. I walked to the stove and flipped the meat just before it burned. The vegetables were sautéing, and the rice was almost done.

"Need a hand?"

"Mine has been working pretty well." I winked and sprinkled more oil over the pan. "Not as good as you though."

She smiled when she understood my meaning. "I guess I should have been more specific. Is there anything I can do to help with dinner?"

"Nah. Take a seat and drink some wine."

She sat on one of the barstools at the counter and poured herself a glass. She stirred the contents before she took a drink. "Pretty good."

"Thanks. I got it for a nickel."

She chuckled. "A BevMo sale?"

"Yep." I tossed the chicken in the pan until it was cooked thoroughly then got the plates ready. I set her plate in front of her and took the seat across from her. I had a dining table, but we never used it. I think I used it one time with Cheyenne, but that was it. It was more for decoration than anything else. When I bought this place, my interior designer picked out everything. She never asked for my opinion because I told her not to bother. I couldn't care less what the place looked like as long as it was masculine. "I bought one bottle and got a few for nearly free. Life is good."

"The little things in life makes us happy."

"Yes, the very little things." I stirred my chicken and rice together before I placed a few pieces in my mouth. I looked across the counter to the beautiful woman sharing a meal with me. I purposely wore a shirt so I wouldn't have to torture her by making her look at my physique. She always had a thing for my shoulders and pecs. "How do you like your food?"

"It's awesome, like everything else you make."

As cheesy as it was, I winked. "I'm the whole package."

She didn't laugh, a serious look on her face as she kept eating. "You really are."

I took another bite but lost my appetite. All I wanted to do was get naked with this woman and wear my heart on my sleeve. I wanted Nathan to be a thing of the past and for me to be her future.

I'd give anything to change things.

"You're the whole package too," I said. "You've got the personality, the humor, and not to mention, the sexiness."

"The sexiness? I'm the least sexy person ever."

"What the hell are you talking about?" I stabbed my fork into my chicken and raised an eyebrow.

"Come on, I told you how I fell in the breakroom at work."

"Happens to the best of us."

"And you know how I am with any kind of fry."

I shrugged. "We all have our weaknesses. Plus, all those things are responsible for your sexiness."

"Really?"

"Yeah. You're real."

Her eyes softened before she looked down at her food. She pushed it around with her fork before she took another bite. "You're sweet."

"No. Just honest."

She stirred her food around before she took another bite. "How was your day?"

"Good. Yours?" I didn't ask what she did with Nathan because I didn't want to know. Madeline covered the major highlights that I needed to know. I needed to focus on getting Austen to understand her feelings for Nathan were just a mix of nostalgia and confusion. There was no way she could take him back after what he did. Zeke made a stupid mistake, but it was out of character. He would never do anything like that again. Plus, he was drunk and heartbroken. Nathan was just a stupid asshole who couldn't keep his dick in his pants.

"Good. Just work. We had pizza in the break room for lunch. That was cool."

"Awesome."

"But I hate it when they give us food because I eat it. And my hips get bigger."

"They get sexier, is what you mean." It was easy to flatter her because my cheesy lines were true. She was painfully beautiful and undeniably perfect."

"I wish bigger was always better, but that's not true in my case."

She'd be sexy at any size. "How's Liam? I haven't talked to him lately."

"I haven't talked to him much either."

Probably because she was spending all her time with Nathan.

"Jared has been sleeping around a lot. I know it's because he can't tell Maddie how he feels."

"Why not?" I asked.

"Her and Liam seem pretty serious. He missed his chance."

"He told you that?"

She nodded. "Yeah. I know he really cares for her. It's too bad things didn't work out."

"You prefer her with your brother?"

She shrugged. "That's hard to answer. Liam is kind of an ass when it comes to women, but he's different with her. I think he's pretty serious. I wish things had worked out for Jared, but if my brother and friend are happy, then I'm happy."

"Poor guy." I hoped I didn't end up like him.

"I'm sure he'll meet another amazing woman. They're everywhere."

"Uh, no," I said with a laugh. "There are women everywhere, but not amazing ones. You're one in a million."

"I don't know about that statistic. Maddie is awesome, and so is Jenn. Boom, that's two chicks right there."

I shook my head. "Your friends are cool, but they've got nothing on you."

She finished her plate, wiping it clean. "I think Madeline is the most beautiful woman I've ever seen. When she dances...she's stunning."

I smiled when I listened to her describe her friend. "You've got a little crush on her?"

"I guess a girl crush."

"Because you totally have my blessing to give that

a go."

She chuckled. "If I were a man, she'd be my first pick. But I'm a woman, and I'm straighter than a rod."

"You're straight for my rod." I waggled my eyebrows.

She was about to drink her wine when she laughed instead. "That's the worst line I've ever heard."

"Trust me, it's not the worst. I can do better than that."

"Geez, I hope not."

I grabbed the plates and set them in the sink. "You wanna watch something?"

"Sure." She moved to the couch with her glass of wine.

I grabbed my own and took the seat directly beside her. It was just her and me in my dimly lit apartment. I set my glass on the end table and wrapped my arm around her shoulders. "What are you in the mood for?"

"A make out session."

The remote was in my hand, and I hit the power button. It took me a second to realize what she said. "Yeah?"

She moved her hand up my chest, feeling the muscled grooves of my body. She leaned into me and pressed her lips to mine, her hair brushing against my neck. She just told me she was the least sexy person in the world, but she was proving how wrong she was. Her hand moved to my shoulder, and she gripped the muscle tightly, her breathing increasing as well as her excitement.

I wasn't sure what was on the TV, but I dropped the remote and listened to it hit the hardwood floor. I guided her down against the couch, her back hitting the cushions. Her hands circled my neck, and she wrapped her legs around my waist.

If she were any other woman, I would be frustrated by the foreplay. I usually wanted to get down to business as quickly as possible, straight fucking and no talking. I could make a woman wet in less than a minute.

But I loved kissing Austen.

It didn't matter if it didn't go anywhere. It didn't matter that I wouldn't get laid. Just being with her was enough for me, to feel her luscious curves pressed against my body. With Austen, it was about more than sex. It was about the two of us together, our tongues moving together like we'd been doing this all our lives.

I should have known she was different the first time I kissed her. I should have known whatever this was was special. I shouldn't have played games and kept her at a distance. The instant I recognized she meant something to me, I should have done whatever I could to keep her.

But I fucked up.

If she ever gave me another chance, I wouldn't fuck up again.

Ever.

Austen

I'd never been so confused in my life.

Every time I was with Ryker, I knew he was the man I wanted to be with. He was the perfect man, minus the fact he was still in love with his ex. He had a good heart, a great sense of humor, and his body was out of this world.

If he wasn't still hung up on Rae, I'd probably pick him.

But he was.

And I still had a thing for Nathan. I went back and forth with him, sometimes wanting to be with him and sometimes wanting to push him away. Sometimes I thought I was just chasing what we used to have. Before he cheated, we had an incredible relationship. He was my best friend and the best lay I'd ever had.

But that was in the past.

Now I was in the present, and I had to make a decision about my future. Whatever man I picked, I'd probably spend the rest of my life with him.

So I needed to choose wisely.

I just got off work when Madeline texted me. *Muffin Girl?*

I could always go for a coffee after work. *Sure. Meet you there in 5.* I walked a few blocks before I found her sitting at the picnic table. She already had two iced coffees and blueberry muffins.

"Hey." I dropped into the bench across from her. "How was practice?"

"Every muscle in my body hurts," she said with a sigh. "But it was worth it. We're gonna be awesome for the opening next week."

"I'll see it myself on opening night."

She smiled before she picked at her muffin. "You always do."

"I'm sure Liam will be there too."

"He's been eager to see one of my shows. He asked to come to practice a few times, but I said no because that would be weird."

"Weird why?"

"All the other girls are practicing, and it's not the

right atmosphere."

"That's probably for the best." I drank my coffee. "He can't handle being around that many pretty girls at one time. His head would explode."

She laughed. "You're probably right. So, who are you seeing tonight? Ryker or Nathan?"

I saw Ryker last night. We made out on the couch then moved into the bedroom. Clothes came off, and there was lots of touching, but no sex. I'd kissed Nathan but we never crossed any lines. "Nathan."

She nodded but didn't hide her look of disappointment. She told me how she felt about Nathan once, but she wouldn't repeat it, not after I asked her not to. "What are you guys doing?"

"Getting dinner and ice cream."

"Cool…" She drank her coffee then stared at her muffins. "Any closer to coming to a decision?"

"I go back and forth a lot." Every time I see each one, actually.

"Is there anything I can do to help your decision?"

"No, I don't think so. I'm running out of time. Maybe when the buzzer goes off, my instinct will make the decision for me."

"Have you done the pros and cons thing?"

"I guess…" They both had equal pros. Their cons were very different.

"What do you like the most about Ryker?"

That was a question that didn't come with a simple answer. "Everything."

"Everything?" she asked with a raised eyebrow. "What does that mean?"

"It means I like everything about him. He's perfect."

"Then what do you like about Nathan?"

I couldn't think of a straight answer. "Everything…"

She laughed. "Well, that didn't help. What about the cons?"

"Well, we know what Nathan's con is…" He slept with my best friend, broke off our engagement, and shattered my heart into a million pieces. "Ryker is still in love with Rae." I could never compete with the only woman he's ever loved.

"Are you sure he is? Because it doesn't seem like it."

"What do you mean?" She was hardly around him.

Madeline considered her answer for a long time before she gave it. "When he's with you, you can tell he's not thinking about someone else. The guy is crazy about you. He has to be if he's going through with this contest."

"I don't doubt his feelings for me." I was just as into him as he was into me. "But I don't want to settle for only some of his heart."

"He's settling for some of yours," she reminded me.

"Which is why it makes even less sense that we

would work out." With Nathan, I seemed to be the only woman in his life.

She crossed her arms and rested her elbows on the table. "I just don't think Ryker is as hung up as you think, so don't assume that."

"And why are you so sure?"

She paused before she answered again. "I just know. I doubt he even thinks about Rae anymore."

I couldn't put much faith in that, not when she hardly knew him. "Hopefully, my answer will come to me. I adore both men, but I'm also nervous to be with either of them."

"Ryker is bluntly obvious. You know exactly what you're getting with him."

"Nathan is honest too."

Madeline wore an irritated look like she didn't agree with that statement. "I know you told me to butt out, but if you let Ryker go, you're going to regret it. Nathan had his chance and blew it."

"Ryker blew his chance too when he hooked up with that bimbo."

"He wasn't in a relationship with you."

"But he didn't care about parading it in my face. He knew it would hurt me, and that's why he did it."

"He only did it because he thought you were getting back together with Nathan. Big difference."

Madeline made her stance on my love life perfectly

clear, and I didn't want to hear it again. "I appreciate your concern. You know I do. But I really need to figure this out on my own."

She rolled her eyes. "Sometimes we need an objective opinion when we're too emotional."

"This is love, Madeline. Of course my decision is emotional."

Madeline finally gave up, the irritation in her eyes. "I just want you to be happy. And I don't think you'll be happy with Nathan. You know what I think—"

"It doesn't matter what you think—"

"You're trying to get back what you had, but it's long gone. You think if you make it work with Nathan, you'll be happy the way you used to. But that can never happen because you're always gonna think about what he did. With Ryker, you get exactly what you expect. He's honest, loyal, and sweet. Don't lose this awesome guy to be with a jerk off."

I bowed my head and let her words wash over me. I shouldn't be angry with her, but I couldn't help it. I needed her support right now, not her ferocity. I'd do anything to be over Nathan so I could move on with my life, but that wasn't so simple. It was wrong of her to judge me like that.

Madeline knew she'd crossed a line. "I'm sorry you're mad at me. I just want the best for you."

"I know..."

"Forget about Nathan, and be with Ryker. He's perfect for you."

I wasn't going to repeat myself—not for the zillionth time. "I know. I'll make my decision soon."

Nathan picked me up, wearing dark jeans and a fitted t-shirt. Every single inch of his body was tight and fit, making him look good in anything he wore. He could wear one of my dresses and still look amazing. "Hey."

"Hi." I locked the door behind me, feeling my throat go dry as the nerves got to me.

His hand moved around my waist, and he leaned in to give me a quick kiss on the lips. "You look nice."

"Thanks…you do too."

He took my hand, and we walked to the restaurant. His thumb brushed over my knuckles as we walked, and his cologne washed over me. Ryker didn't wear cologne. He always smelled like the body wash he used in the shower. It was heavy in all of his sheets. Nathan had been wearing the same cologne since the first day I met him.

I tried not to think about Ryker. That wasn't fair to Nathan.

"Hungry?" he asked.

"Starving. I did ten thousand steps at work today."

"Wow. That's a lot. That treadmill desk really works."

"Yeah. They're starting to put them in the rest of the offices. I think it's good for everyone."

"I'm sure it will be."

We arrived at the restaurant and were led to our seats. Nathan made reservations, and it was a good thing he did because the place was packed. It was swanky like all the other places he took me. I wasn't sure if he had expensive taste or if he was just trying to impress me. Ryker and I usually got burgers when we were together, or even better, pizza. We were pretty simple. "This place looks nice."

"I heard it's good."

"My parents like this place." I saw the name of the restaurant on the wall and remembered my mom talking about it.

"Seems like something they'd like. They have steak, and your dad loves that."

"He loves it too much, actually. His cholesterol is off the charts."

"Nothing will stand in the way between a man and his meat."

I chuckled then looked at the menu.

The waiter came over and took our drink orders before he disappeared again.

"What are you going to get?" Nathan closed his menu like he had already decided.

"All this talk about meat makes me paranoid. I'll get some fish."

"Isn't that meat?" he asked with a laugh.

"But it's good meat. Now I won't feel so bad about it." I closed my menu and placed it on top of his.

The waiter came over, and we ordered before he disappeared again.

Once he was gone, the air became heavy with tension. Nathan kept staring at me, his eyes glued to my face. We were just joking around a moment ago, but now everything seemed different. "I don't want to ask this, but my curiosity is getting the best of me."

He could only be referring to one person.

"You've been seeing both of us for a while now. Are you still unsure of your answer?"

It'd been over two weeks. I didn't have much time left. "It's complicated…"

"Is Ryker still in love with his ex?"

Thinking about him and Rae still made me sick. "As far as I know."

He nodded slowly. "Well, I'm only in love with one person…"

The confession sent chills down my spine and butterflies into my stomach. I remembered the way he always told me he loved me before he left for work in the morning. I missed those little moments, things I took for granted at the time.

"And I know you love me." He rested his hand on the table, directly next to the glass of scotch he wasn't drinking. "With me, you don't have to compete with anyone. All I want is you."

While it was sweet, all I could think about was Lily. "It's not so simple. You know you really hurt me, Nathan."

"I know," he whispered. "But I'll never make that mistake again."

I believed him even though I had no reason to. I felt the sweat collect on the back of my neck, so I massaged the area to discreetly wipe it away. When Nathan turned that stare on me, I felt powerless to do anything about it. He was pressuring me to choose him when he'd been nothing but patient for the past few weeks. His jealousy was obviously getting to him. "I know. I just—"

"Austen?" I could recognize that voice in a crowded room. With grace and a hint of shrillness, my mother's voice pierced my eardrum.

I looked up to see her standing there beside my father, wearing one of her nice dresses with a clutch tucked under her arm. My father stood beside her in a collared shirt, tall just like Liam. He and my mother both looked at Nathan in shock, their eyes wide and full of horror.

It took me a moment to respond because I hadn't recovered from the last thing Nathan said. "Hey…what are you guys doing here?" It was a stupid question because I knew exactly why they were there. I knew they liked that restaurant, but I never thought we would cross paths.

My parents never responded to the question. Their eyes were reserved for Nathan.

Nathan was the first one to make a move. He cleared his throat and stood up. "Nice to see you again, sir." He stuck out his hand to shake my father's.

My father stared him down and didn't move. He was always polite to everyone he interacted with. He had a high tolerance for bullshit, and it was nearly impossible to make him mad. The fact he stood still like a statue was clear evidence of how he felt.

Nathan held his hand for a few more seconds before he dropped it. "Nice to see you, Melinda…"

With pursed lips and threatening eyes, she stared at Nathan like he was a bug. She eventually turned back to me, a questioning look in her eyes. "I'll call you tomorrow, sweetheart." She stepped away and didn't look at Nathan again.

My father stared him down, looking threatening when I didn't think it was possible. He was in his fifties and possessed a friendly visage. But right now, he was a little scary. "You have a lot of nerve." He followed my mother out the door and to the lobby.

I wanted to apologize for my parents' behavior, but I

E. L. TODD

couldn't. They had every right to be angry, especially since my dad lost half his deposit for the wedding venue that was never used. My mother lost a lot of money on the wedding dress she never got to see her daughter wear. And after the way he broke my heart, it was no surprise my parents didn't possess an ounce of forgiveness.

Nathan watched them go before he slowly lowered himself into his chair. He leaned back with slumped shoulders, looking like he lost a hand he shouldn't have gambled in the first place. He ran his fingers through his hair and sighed.

I didn't know what to say to make him feel better. In reality, I really shouldn't need to make him feel better at all. The last time he saw my parents, we had brunch together and talked about wedding plans. My father adored him, would take him fishing all the time. But they hadn't spoken since Liam moved out and chose to be with Lily. It was a cold reminder of what he'd done, not just to me, but my entire family.

Since I couldn't think of anything to say, I didn't say anything at all.

Nathan stared at the tabletop, his eyes heavy and lifeless. "I guess I deserved that…"

I wasn't surprised when my mom called me the next day. She called the second I walked out of the building, knowing exactly when I got off work and was free to talk. I knew this conversation was coming, so I didn't bother sighing before I answered the phone. "Hey, Mom."

She didn't greet me with normal pleasantries. Normally, she asked how work was going or if I had any fun plans for the evening. It was always easy talk, subjects that didn't make anyone uncomfortable. But the mama bear inside her came out, claws and teeth showing. "Hey, sweetheart. Your father and I were very surprised when we saw you with Nathan last night." Without asking a single question, she interrogated me. It was a talent every single mom possessed.

"Yeah, I know."

"I was hoping you were dating that nice young man, Ryker." Another loaded question.

"I was...I still am."

"If you're seeing Ryker, then why were you having dinner with Nathan?" she pressed.

"I'm kinda dating both of them."

My mom knew I wasn't a two-timer. "And they're okay with that?"

"Yeah, I'm supposed to pick the guy I like most in a few weeks." I totally sounded like a slut, but whatever.

Mom paused for a long time before she spoke. "You

know I've never given you any direction when it comes to your love life. Your father and I always mind our own business. But this is something we can't be quiet about. After what Nathan did to you…to us…we don't want him anywhere near you."

"I know…"

"Why on earth would you date him again?"

I'd been getting that question a lot. "I don't know… I still love him."

"Well, he obviously didn't love you," she snapped. "That man hurt all of us. He's not good enough for you, Austen. No man is perfect, but some men are more flawed than others. Nathan doesn't deserve a second chance. Your father and I can't watch you go through that again."

"I know…"

"So you really need to think about what you're doing."

I hated being bossed around by my mother. Every daughter did. But in this case, she had every right to say this to me. When I hurt, so did she. When Nathan broke my heart, he broke her heart too. She wanted me to end up with someone great, someone who would take care of me for the rest of my life. But Nathan broke their trust as well as mine. "I know."

"I'm sorry to be so harsh. It's just…your father is never going to get over what happened. Neither will I."

"I forgave him. It wasn't easy, but I did. When he apologized, he seemed sincere. I couldn't live the rest of my life being so angry. I kept it built up inside and let it control my life. I was lost for so long...I needed to let it go."

My mom sighed into the phone. "Forgiveness is good. We should always forgive and forget. But we should also learn from our mistakes, learn from our pain. Nathan did something terrible. I don't think he's a horrible human being, but he's definitely not good enough for you. You can't spend the rest of your life with a man who would ever cross a line like that."

I bowed my head and stood off to the side of the sidewalk. People passed as they headed home from work, looking down at their phones or speeding down the pavement on their way to the gym or the bar.

"Are you still there, Austen?"

"Yeah, Mom." I was surprised Liam hadn't already told them I was talking to Nathan again. My brother could be a jerk that didn't know when to back off, but I appreciated that he wasn't a rat. He never tattled on me, even when we were little. That was something I always appreciated.

"I always told myself I wouldn't be one of those mothers. You know, the kind that bosses their grown daughter around. I hate talking to you like this, giving you my opinion about such an important decision. But I love you. I just want the best for you."

How could I be mad when she only had good intentions? "I know, Mom. I understand. I'd probably be the same way if I had a kid."

"You've always been so mature. Not sure what I did to get two great kids."

"You raised us right. That's how."

Mom lightened up at the compliment. "Thanks, honey. I hope you really think this through. Of course, your father and I will respect whatever decision you make. I just hope you make the right one."

RAE

I walked through the door and was greeted by Safari and Razor. With both of their tongues hanging out and their eyes lit up with joy, they greeted me like they'd been thinking about me all day. "Hey, boys." I set my purse down then kneeled so I could give both of them a good rub down. "Missed you."

Rex's voice came from the living room. "Take that, sucker." The sound of the video game blared from the TV. They were probably racing each other on a new car racing video game that Zeke just picked up.

"I lapped you already, idiot," Zeke said back. "You're still behind me."

"Ah, shit," Rex snapped.

I rolled my eyes then walked into the living room.

Rex had hung out at the house all day yesterday playing this stupid game. Zeke barely paid any attention to me until Rex finally left at ten o'clock. But we just had sex then went to sleep. I didn't give him a hard time about it because I didn't care if he spent a lot of time with Rex once a week. But two days in a row? That was a little much. "Hi."

Rex tilted the controller as he rounded a curve. "Pedal to the metal…"

"I said hi," I repeated.

Rex kept his eyes glued to the screen. "Yeah, whatever."

"Whatever what?" I snapped. "You're in my house. Just say hi back."

"I'm in Zeke's house," Rex argued. "Get it right."

I placed both hands on my hips and glared at the back of his head.

Zeke hit the pause button then stood up. "Hey, baby."

"Goddammit." Rex dropped his controller on the cushion next to him. "We're in the middle of a game."

"It can wait." Zeke walked toward me in his jeans and white t-shirt. He showered when he got home from work, and his hair was still a little damp because he didn't dry it. Rex must have been waiting for him so he didn't want to spend any extra time getting ready. The smile on his face went straight to my stomach. His eyes were lit up with affection, and he was eager to see me.

His arms moved around my waist, and he kissed me. "Missed you."

My arms circled his neck, and I kissed him again, missing him now that I was competing for his affection. "I missed you too."

"Yuck." Rex stared straight ahead so he wouldn't have to look at us.

"Get used to it, asshole," I barked. "Or leave."

"Why don't you go in your bedroom?" Rex snapped.

"Why don't you go home?" I countered.

Rex didn't have an argument against that. "Hurry up and kiss your woman. We've gotta finish this race."

Zeke hugged me to his chest and gave me another squeeze. "Have a good day at work?"

"It was alright," I said. "Just another day of garbage and microbes."

"Saucy," he said with a smile.

"What's for dinner?" Rex turned around and looked at me from his spot on the couch.

I glared at him. "Why do you ask me that?"

"Because you belong in the kitchen," Rex said with a straight face. "That's why."

Zeke grabbed both of my wrists before I could smack him upside the head. "You know he's kidding."

"No, I'm not." Rex turned back around. "Kayden can bring something by. She usually cooks."

If I didn't love my brother so much, I would murder

him. "I was gonna make tacos tonight—for the two of us."

Rex turned back around. "For real? Man, I love your tacos. That sautéed ground beef with the taco sauce and fresh tomatoes…heaven."

It was a compliment, but I didn't take it that way. "Who said anything about you having dinner with us?"

"Oh, come on," Rex said. "I've made you dinner loads of times."

"Have not." I crossed my arms over my chest.

"When you and Zeke broke up, I cooked for you every night. Don't act like you don't remember that."

I quickly remembered all the trouble Rex went through to make sure I kept eating. But that was a different circumstance. "Did you and Kayden break up?"

"No," Rex blurted. "You think I'd let that hot little number go?"

"Then I'm not cooking for you." I wanted to move into Zeke's body again, but having my brother sitting there and watching made me uncomfortable.

"Fine." Rex turned back around. "I'll order a pizza."

Zeke grabbed my hand and pulled me into the kitchen. "You really want me to kick him out?" He kept his voice low so Rex wouldn't hear.

Yes, I wanted to spend the evening with just Zeke and the dogs. I cherished nights when it was just the two of us. But I knew I spent a lot of time with Kayden and

Jessie, so it would be hypocritical of me to make a big deal out of it. "No. But tomorrow, you're mine."

"That sounds fair." He backed me up into the counter and gave me a kiss that wasn't meant for an audience. His hands moved underneath my shirt, and he felt my tits through my bra, squeezing them with perfect pressure. His cock hardened in his jeans, and he pressed it right against my hip.

He reluctantly pulled away, his hands wanting to continue to explore. "Should I order a pizza?"

"No, I'll cook."

Zeke smiled, preferring my cooking to anything we could order. "Great. Need any help?"

"No. You have fun with your friend."

His hands squeezed my hips. "You're the best. You know that?"

"I thought I was the best because I give great blow jobs."

He grinned. "It certainly helps."

When Rex finally left, we got to spend some alone time together. We had sex on the couch, my leg hooked over his shoulder. He gave it to me good and hard, bringing me to a climax that hurt the dogs' ears.

Then we went to the bedroom together and did our

nightly routine. I washed my face then lay in bed. Zeke sat up and read on his Kindle, looking through published research in dermatology. He never read fiction for pleasure, always choosing to focus on factual information in his field.

I wouldn't want to read about cystic acne before bed.

When Zeke saw me staring at him, he turned to me. Shirtless and with messy hair, he looked sexy right before bed. He looked sexy in the morning too. Come to think of it, he looked sexy no matter what time of the day it was. "What?"

"What?" I countered. "I can't just look at you?"

He turned back to his Kindle. "Seems like something is on your mind."

"Rex is a little annoying…"

"It seems like something bigger than that."

There had been something on my mind. "I've been thinking about Ryker a lot…" The mention of his name used to really piss Zeke off. It made him so angry he couldn't see straight. But now that Ryker was into Austen and on the other side of the country, he didn't seem to care. We were living together and blissfully happy. There was no reason to be jealous about anything.

He knew this conversation wouldn't end quickly, so he set his Kindle on his nightstand. "What do you mean?"

"About this Austen girl. The way he talks about her… seems like he's really into her."

"Probably is."

"He claims I'm the reason he's holding back…but I don't think I'm a problem anymore."

"Meaning?" he asked.

"He says he still has feelings for me…but I don't think he does."

Zeke turned off the lamp at his bedside. It brought the room into darkness but we could still see each other clearly. "I think a man knows how he feels."

"I think he just assumes he feels that way. But if he really did, he wouldn't be so hung up on her. I think she's replaced me in his heart, but he doesn't realize it. And I wish he did."

He shrugged. "Sounds complicated."

"Not really. And now she's seeing that other guy…I wish I could fix it for him."

"Fix it?"

"Yeah. Bring them together so they can be happy. I'm worried Ryker is gonna blow this and be miserable for a long time. He's very picky when it comes to women, and I'm afraid he's never gonna find another incredible person. I don't want him to be alone. I want him to have what we have."

Zeke shook his head. "I have to say, Rochelle would

never care about my happiness the way you care about his."

I shrugged. "I love him…as a friend." Ryker and I used to be really close. Now that I was in love with someone else, my feelings for him had changed. He was still important to me, just in a different way. "I want him to be happy."

Zeke adjusted his pillows then lay back on the bed. His hand rested on his stomach and he turned his head so he could look at me. "You're always fixing people. It's cute."

"I'm not sure why I'm like that."

"Maybe because you and Rex had to take care of each other when you were young. You're the mother hen."

"Maybe."

"But I'm not sure how you can fix Ryker's life. He's on the other side of the country." He turned his head and faced the ceiling again. He usually fell asleep pretty early in the evening since he woke up so early. He headed to the gym then worked directly afterward.

An idea popped into my head. "What if I go there and help him?"

"What?" he asked with a laugh. "You mean, go to New York?"

"Yeah. I can have girl talk with Austen."

"I doubt she wants to see you in person," he said. "That'll just make her more jealous."

"Why?"

He rolled his eyes. "Because she'll see how hot you are. That's why."

"Oh, shut up." I smacked his arm. "Just because you find me attractive doesn't mean the whole world does."

"Trust me, the whole world does."

"Anyway, if I just talk to her, maybe I can make her choose Ryker and forget about that other guy."

"I suspect Ryker wouldn't be happy if he knew about this."

"So what?" I asked. "If it works, what does it matter?"

"But what if you make things worse?"

I would hate myself if I did. "I have to do something. I have to convince Austen that he doesn't love me anymore. If that's the only reason why she doesn't want to be with him, then she needs to know the truth. She could pick the wrong guy, and Ryker will be miserable forever."

Zeke sighed like this conversation was boring him. "So you're serious?"

"Dead serious."

"You want all of us to go there?"

"Who said anything about all of us?" I asked. "I can just go. I'll leave on Friday after work."

"You know we'll be totally helpless without you. We won't know what to do with ourselves."

"Shut up, you'll be fine." Kayden could cook for Rex, and Zeke knew how to survive before I came along.

"I want to come along. Maybe I can help."

"Rex can't help. He'll just make things worse."

"He's always wanted to go to New York. Says he wants to try the other Mega Shake to compare."

Rex was the biggest idiot on the planet. "It's an expensive trip just to interfere with Ryker's love life."

"So what? It could be fun. Maybe we can help."

"You might be able to help," I said. "Rex will just say something stupid."

"You know, some of the stupid things he says are helpful."

"How?" I asked incredulously.

"It doesn't matter how bad the situation is. That guy can always make you laugh."

"What are we gonna do first?" Rex asked. "Statue of Liberty? The Empire State Building? Strip club?" He grabbed his bag from the baggage claim and hoisted it over his shoulder.

Kayden gave him a dirty look. "No strip club. You want a stripper? I'll oblige."

Rex's face lit up like Christmas morning. "That

would be the best thing ever. What hotel are we staying at?"

I walked away with Zeke so I wouldn't have to listen to the details of their strange sex life. "Let's take our stuff to the hotel then meet Austen."

"How are we going to do that?" Zeke walked beside me, holding his bag as well as mine. "We don't know where she lives. We don't even have her number."

"Maybe we can look her up?"

"Do you know her last name?"

"Uh…no." I doubt Ryker ever told me.

"Maybe we should have thought this through before we traveled across the country." Zeke was never thrilled about this plan, but came along to be supportive. When he tried to make things right with Rochelle, I was on board. I'd do anything for him, and he always did anything for me.

"We'll figure it out. I can tell Ryker I'm in town and we can hang out. I'll get her number from his phone."

"That's pretty 007."

"Yeah, I know."

"But maybe you should just ask for her number. Or it's kind of a breach of privacy."

"No. If Ryker knew what I was planning, he would tell me to go home."

Zeke nodded. "And for good reason."

211

"I'm not turning back now. If I can do some good for him, I will. He deserves to be happy."

Zeke sat at the desk with his laptop out. He was checking his emails since he skipped work that day. He moved some of his appointments around and even referred a few to one of his colleagues so we could make the early flight. I told him he could stay behind, but he didn't want to.

We heard a loud thump from next door.

Zeke looked up from the email he was reading. "Rex and Kayden seem to be enjoying the room…"

"Why did they put us right next to each other?"

"Probably because both rooms were charged to the same credit card."

"Lesson learned." I pulled out my phone and pulled up Ryker's number. "Alright, here goes nothing…"

"Good luck." Zeke turned back to his computer right when another thud sounded.

I walked to the wall then slammed my fist against it, thinking that would shut them up.

Of course, Rex purposely made another thud just to annoy me.

Zeke shook his head. "Baby, just leave it alone. You're going to start a war that you'll never finish."

I sighed and made the call.

Ryker answered after a few rings. "Hey, Rae. To what do I owe the pleasure?" Ryker had a naturally sexy voice. He could read audiobooks for a living if he wanted to. He sounded both confident and playful at the same time.

"I have a big surprise for you."

"Hmm…you sent me an Edible Arrangement?"

"No…"

"You got another dog?"

He would never guess it. "How about I just tell you? I'm in New York right now. Rex, Zeke, Kayden and I decided to take a quick trip to the city."

"Seriously?" The smile was heavy in his voice. "That's awesome. We have to meet up. I can take you to all the great local spots, none of those tourist trap places."

"Yeah, that'd be great. Are you free tonight?"

"As a matter of fact, I am."

"Perfect. We'll meet you at seven?"

"Sure thing."

"Are you gonna bring Austen along?" If he brought her, that would make things easier. He had to go to the bathroom sometime, and I could make my little speech.

"No." His buoyant attitude dropped immediately. "She has plans tonight."

I had a feeling I knew with who. "We'll meet you then. The gang is excited to see you."

"And I'm always excited to see them." He hung up.

I tossed my phone on the bed. "We're gonna see him at seven."

Zeke closed his laptop like he was finished. "I know, I heard. That gives us a few hours. What should we do?" He rose out of his chair and came toward me, his strong arms swinging by his sides.

"Hmm... I don't have any ideas."

"I do." He stopped when he was directly in front of me, his face just inches from mine. His confidence was naturally sexy, the way he carried himself with authority. I liked to be the one in charge, but whenever Zeke did it, I always yielded.

He pushed me onto the bed then pulled his shirt over his head. A powerful physique with an eight pack was revealed, chiseled and defined like a statue made out of marble. He yanked my shoes off then undid my jeans, doing it as quickly but calmly as possible.

I was eager for him to be inside me, to feel that wonderful stretch that always made me feel like a woman.

He pulled my jeans and panties off and didn't bother with my top. He removed his own bottoms and shoes and crawled on top of me, his hard cock ready for me. I didn't think about anything else but the two of us. Ryker wasn't on my mind, and neither was Rex and Kayden. It was just the two of us.

Together.

We found Ryker in the bar sitting in a booth. He had a beer in front of him. In a red t-shirt and dark jeans, he looked exactly the way I remembered. He stood up when he saw us and pasted a genuine smile on his lips. "There's the gang." He hugged me first, the kind of embrace that was purely friendly. It was quick before he moved on to the next person, shaking Zeke's hand before hugging Kayden.

I watched Rex fist-bump him. They were definitely making progress.

We took a seat in the booth and ordered our beers. Judging by the looks of the bar, it was definitely a place for locals. There were TVs on most of the walls along with signed jerseys from the Yankees. The owner must know someone associated with the team.

Rex chugged his beer like he hadn't had a drink all day. "Ice-cold beer...nothing better."

"Had a long day?" Ryker asked.

"That flight was long as hell," Rex answered. "I've never traveled that far before."

"Take some Nyquil on the way home and sleep through it," Ryker suggested. "Makes the flight a lot shorter that way."

Rex gave him a thumbs up. "Noted."

"How long are you guys here for?" Ryker asked.

"Just the weekend," I answered.

Ryker raised an eyebrow before he took a drink. "That's a short trip."

"We just wanted to get out of Seattle," I lied. "You know, all the rain gets old."

"I thought you liked the rain?" Ryker asked.

"I do," I said. "But it's been raining a lot lately. Like, too much. I haven't been able to take the dogs out much, and they're pretty miserable."

"Poor guys," Ryker said. "How are the pups doing?"

"Good." I smiled when I thought about our two dogs. "Safari is really happy having someone to play with. He has someone to hang out with all day while Zeke and I are working."

"That's how I would like it if I were a dog," Ryker said. "I'd want a buddy."

I wasn't sure how to get his phone from him. If he went to the bathroom, he'd probably keep his phone in his pocket. I'd have to get his phone on the table before he walked away. "What's new with you?"

"Nothing really," he answered. "I'm waiting for Austen to make up her mind. She's still seeing Nathan… and I keep pretending to be okay with it."

"There's no way she can choose him over you." She would be stupid to pick a cheating asshole over one of the most amazing men in the world.

He shrugged. "She's been dating him for nearly three weeks now. She's obviously seriously considering him."

Not after I spoke to her. "Can I see her picture again?" It was a lame excuse, but Ryker might go for it.

"You forgot what she looks like?" he asked as he pulled his phone out.

"No. Just want to see her again, that's all." I tried to act normal even though that was difficult. If I had a trick up my sleeve, I wasn't very good at hiding it.

Ryker pulled up a different picture and slid the phone toward me. "I took that when I made dinner the other night. I liked the way she looked in that dress."

I gave Rex a meaningful look before I stared at the picture. It was a candid photo. She was standing in front of the window in the main room, and she just turned around to look at him. He caught her at the perfect moment, partially candid and partially staged. She was definitely beautiful.

Kayden discreetly swatted Rex's hand on the table.

He set his beer down in a hurry, and spilled some across the table. "Dude, let's hit the restroom. I've gotta take a leak."

Ryker stared at him with a raised eyebrow, like he wasn't sure if Rex was talking to him.

"Yeah, me too." Zeke stood up too, probably trying to help in whatever way he could. "You coming, Ryker?"

Ryker glanced at both of them. "Uh, I'm good. Don't

need to pee. But thanks for the concern…" He turned back to his phone and changed the picture. "Here's another one I got of her."

Rex looked at Zeke and shrugged. Zeke rubbed the back of his head, trying to figure out what to do.

Rex tried again. "Dude, you know it's bad to hold your pee. Not good for the bladder and stuff."

"What?" Ryker asked. "That's not true."

"Yeah, it is," Zeke lied. "You've never heard that?"

Good thing Zeke was a doctor.

"But I'm not holding it," Ryker said. "I just—"

"Just come to the bathroom with us," Rex snapped. "This is New York City. I'm a little scared to move around alone, alright? Thanks for putting me on the spot."

"Isn't Zeke going with you?" Ryker asked.

"But he's a doctor," Rex said. "He might be able to save my life if I get in a bad fight. But he's not good backup, you know?"

This was the stupidest conversation I'd ever heard.

Ryker finally gave up. "Fine, I'll come with you." Ryker left the table and walked away with the guys.

The second his back was turned, I snatched his phone.

"There's no way Ryker believed any of that," Kayden said. "Only an idiot would."

"I could tell the only reason why Ryker left was to get

them to shut up. But whatever, it worked." I hit the home button, and the screen lit up.

But there was a passcode.

God fucking dammit. "Shit."

"Maybe it's his birthday?"

I typed it in the numbers, but that didn't work. "I hate Ryker so much right now."

"Maybe it's something simple, like 1,2,3,4."

That didn't work either. "No…"

"Didn't his dad pass away? Maybe it's his birthday."

"I have no idea when his dad's birthday is."

"Then we're shit out of luck," Kayden said.

I stared at the numbers on the screen and knew I would never break into his phone. But by a stroke of luck, Austen texted him.

You wanna get breakfast tomorrow?

"She texted him."

Kayden leaned over and looked at the screen. "Perfect. Say you'll meet her."

"What?"

"Yeah. That way we can show up instead and talk to her."

Actually, that was perfect. I texted her back. *Yeah, when and where?*

How about Cindy's Diner?

That works for me. See you then, baby.

Baby?

"Shit, he must not call her that."

"Think," Kayden said. "Didn't he call you sweetheart all the time?"

"That's true." *I'll see you in the morning, sweetheart.*

K.

"Phew, that was close." I used baby because that's what Zeke called me all the time.

"Should you erase the messages?"

"I can't erase them without erasing all of the messages. And that will be really obvious."

"What if she texts him and cancels?"

"Then we're screwed. Hopefully, she won't." I turned off the screen and returned the phone to where it was. "He knows she has plans tonight, so I doubt he'll text her."

"Let's hope not. Otherwise our plan is totally ruined."

"Maybe you should just go on your own," Zeke said. "It's a bit of a difficult conversation."

"He might be right," Kayden said. "She might feel bombarded with four people ganging up on her."

"We aren't ganging up on her," I said. "We're just talking. And I think if she sees me with Zeke, I'll be less threatening to her. I've moved on, and I'm obviously happy. There's no possibility of Ryker and I getting back together. And if we go as a group, she'll see that we're all friends. It might make her more comfortable."

Zeke exchanged a look with Rex then shrugged. "Yeah, maybe. But I'd be pretty freaked out if a group of four strangers sat at my table and talked to me like they knew me when we've never met."

"I'm sure it'll be fine." From the way Ryker described her, she seemed like a tough cookie. It would take a lot more than the four of us to scare her.

"I hope this works," Zeke said. "Otherwise, you might just make things worse for Ryker."

That was something I hadn't anticipated.

Zeke watched me with his typical handsome gaze, waiting for me to think this through.

"But I know if I do nothing, I'm definitely not helping him. I have to at least try."

Zeke knew I'd made my decision, so he didn't try to talk me out of it anymore. "Alright, let's do this thing."

We met Rex and Kayden in the hallway. They were bickering back and forth.

"We don't have time to do both," Kayden said. "Pick one. Statue of Liberty or the Empire State Building."

"We can totally do both," Rex argued.

"We're leaving tomorrow."

"We'll stop by before we head to the airport," he said.

"It's gonna be a zoo," Kayden argued. "It's not like

swinging by the grocery store and picking up a few things."

"So we flew all the way here and didn't get to see anything?" Rex asked incredulously.

"We got to see Ryker," Kayden reminded him.

He gave her a stoic stare before he rolled his eyes. "Yeah…that made it all worthwhile."

If I didn't interrupt them, this was going to go on forever. "Guys, we're meeting Austen for breakfast. We all need to be on our best behavior." Kayden and Zeke were fine. I was only referring to one person without singling him out.

"Best behavior?" Rex asked. "Are we children?"

I stared him down. "Some of us are."

"Oh, that's how it is?" he challenged. "I come all the way here to help you and you—"

"You came here for a free vacation," I countered. "The sooner we talk to Austen, the sooner we're free to do whatever we want."

"Don't you think Ryker is gonna be angry about this?" Zeke asked.

"Not if we get them together," I said. "He'll thank us on his hands and knees. So, are we ready to do this?"

"I'm in," Zeke said. "Operation Cupid." He put his hand in the center of the circle.

Rex did the same thing and rested his hand on Zeke's. "Operation Cupid."

Kayden crossed her arms over her chest and stared at the two men. "It looks like you guys are holding hands. It's cute."

"Eww." Rex quickly yanked his hand away. "We were doing a team huddle. We weren't holding hands."

"It looked like you were holding hands," Kayden said. "And it looked like you liked it too."

Zeke shrugged. "You caught me. I'm only dating Rae to get closer to him."

Rex officially had enough. "Okay, this is starting to freak me out. Let's get this shit taken care of so we can get home."

"No more Statue of Liberty?" Kayden asked with a laugh.

Rex kept walking. "Let's just stop by Mega Shake, and I'll be happy."

***

The four of us walked into the diner and looked around.

"Where is she?" Rex asked.

I looked to the left side of the restaurant but didn't spot her anywhere. "Maybe she's not here yet."

Zeke looked to the right. "I think she's over there. Dark hair, right?"

She was sitting near the back of the restaurant with dark hair that was in loose curls. She was looking down at her phone with a steaming mug of coffee next to her. "Yeah, that's her."

"Hopefully, she's not texting Ryker," Rex said. "That would be bad for all of us."

I led the charge and walked to her table, knowing she was going to be alarmed when I first sat down. She kept looking at her phone as she drank her coffee, oblivious to the ambush coming her way.

I slid into the opposite side of the booth and felt her eyes shift to my face. The rest of the gang scooted in beside me, squeezing into the cramped space.

Austen looked at all of us, her eyebrows raised and her fingers still wrapped around the handle of her coffee mug. "Uh…do I know you?"

"No," Rex said. "But everything will make sense in just a few seconds. Rae?" He turned to me, giving me the stage to make my case.

Her eyes turned back to me. "Rae? As in…Ryker's Rae?"

I hoped that reference wouldn't piss off Zeke. His jealousy had vanished, but it wouldn't take much to stir it up again. "Yeah, I guess." Now that I was face to face with her, I was nervous. All I wanted was for Ryker to have what I had. I wanted him to be happy, to get married and have lots of kids with a special woman. I wanted him to have what I had with Zeke, a partner that would always look after him. "Ryker doesn't know I'm here. I took his phone last night and texted you."

"Oh…" Her gaze shifted to everyone else before she turned back to me. "Okay…I still don't understand."

"Well, let me begin by introducing Zeke." I pointed to him right beside me. "He's my boyfriend. We've been together for a while, and we're really happy together." I pointed at Rex. "That's my brother, Rex."

Rex waved. "Yes, it's true. We're somehow related."

I pointed to Kayden. "And that's Rex's girlfriend, Kayden. She's also my friend."

"Uh, hi." Austen gave an awkward wave. "I guess you all know who I am. So, why did you want to meet me?"

"To talk about Ryker." She must have figured that out despite the fact she asked the question. "He talks about you pretty often."

"He does?" she whispered.

"Yeah. You're all he ever talks about, actually," I said with a chuckle. "He's pretty head-over-heels for you."

"He doesn't wear heels," Rex corrected. "So let's just say he's crazy about you."

"Very crazy about you," Zeke added.

Austen listened to both of them before she turned back to me.

"I know you're dating Nathan too while you try to decide who you should be with…but I think it would be a mistake not to pick Ryker." I was giving a complete stranger love advice, but she might take it. "He's an incredible man. You can't go wrong with him. He's honest, caring, sweet, sexy...he's everything." I knew Zeke wouldn't be happy about that last comment, but hopefully he'd let it slide.

Austen didn't show a hint of jealousy. "I know he's perfect. He's only been in my life for four months, but I feel like I've known him forever."

"Then don't waste your time with Nathan, not after what he did to you."

She tucked her hair behind her ear. "It's a lot more complicated than that."

"It's not complicated at all." I needed to tone it down, but I couldn't help myself. "I don't know Nathan and I don't know what your relationship is like, but I can guarantee this guy has nothing on Ryker. He's the better guy."

"He probably is the better guy. But there's a huge problem in the mix."

"What?" I asked.

She gave me a firm look. "You know exactly what the problem is. And now that I know what you look like, I can't blame him for still being in love with you. You're even prettier than I feared."

The compliment meant nothing to me in that moment. "He was in love with me, but he's not anymore."

"That's not what he told me."

"He just thinks he's in love with me. But I can guarantee you he's not."

"And how would you know?" she asked. "You know him better than he knows himself?"

"Pretty much," I answered. "All he ever talks about is you. He shows me pictures of you on his phone, ones where you're sleeping or not paying attention. When he describes you…you can tell."

Rex nodded. "I noticed it too. He's totally into you."

"And he doesn't look at Rae the way he used to," Zeke said. "I've seen it with my own eyes. And I'm pretty jealous when it comes to the guy, so you know I'm being honest."

I watched Austen soak everything in, listening to us argue on Ryker's behalf. "He doesn't want you to be with Nathan. You dating both of them is killing him. Every time you're with Nathan, he can't sleep because he can't stand the thought of that guy touching you. He regrets letting it get this far. He wishes he'd snatched you when he had a chance. Believe me, he's not thinking about me anymore."

She grabbed the handle of her mug but didn't take a drink. She stared at us with indecision in her eyes. The steam continued to rise to the ceiling because she hadn't cooled it down with creamer. "You came all the way to New York just to tell me this?"

I nodded. "Ryker is family to us. We want him to be happy."

"Wow, that's really sweet," she said. "All my friends love him too."

"I understand what it's like to want to go back to your ex." I was thinking of Ryker, and everyone at the table knew I was. "I wanted to have what we used to have too once. But, I found someone else that made me happy, and I knew it was right. Sometimes we want to go back in time and feel those emotions again, but we just can't. When it's over, it's over. We have to move on. I don't know Nathan, but I don't need to know him. He's not the right guy. Ryker is."

Austen listened to everything I said with soft eyes. "I've always known it wouldn't work with Nathan. Sometimes I pretend to myself that it could…sometimes I try to give myself closure after what happened. Ryker is the one I'm always thinking about. He's the one that makes me laugh, makes me happy. I guess I've always kept my distance because…of you."

I wished I could rewrite history to make Ryker's life easier. I wished we'd never had our time together so he could have found Austen sooner. I didn't regret our relationship, but I wished everything was simpler. "I'm not a problem anymore. He's over me, Austen. It may be hard to believe, but I know he is."

"How?" she pressed.

"When I saw him last night, he didn't hug me the way he used to. It was quick and simple, just how he hugged Kayden. His eyes didn't linger on my face. He didn't pay any special attention to me. Every time he looked away, sadness filled his eyes because he was thinking about you. That's how I know."

Austen finally took a drink of her coffee, giving herself an instant to compose herself.

"Forget about Nathan," I said. "Pick Ryker. I promise you'll regret it if you don't."

She set her mug down and finally nodded. "Yeah, I know."

Did that mean I succeeded? "So...you're going to talk to him?"

"Yeah," she whispered. "I think so."

"Really?" I couldn't stop the smile from spreading across my lips. "You're gonna call it off with Nathan?"

She nodded again. "Every time I'm with Nathan, I think about Ryker. But when I'm with Ryker, I never think about Nathan. That's how I know he's the right one. I guess I've just been scared to be the lesser choice in his eyes...but after meeting you and talking to you, I think everything will be okay."

I wanted to throw my fist into the air to celebrate. "That's so great."

"Awesome," Rex said. "He's a hottie, so you made the right choice."

Austen stared at him with a raised eyebrow.

"He's totally straight," Kayden said. "I can vouch for that."

"Of course I'm straight," Rex argued. "I'm just stating the obvious. He's a good-looking guy."

"Well, I don't think he's good-looking," Zeke said. "He's just a dude to me."

"So, when are you going to talk to him?" I asked.

"Well, I should probably talk to Nathan first," she said. "That would be the right thing to do."

"Yeah, probably." I wanted her to skip that conversation and go straight to Ryker. The sooner he was happy, the sooner I would be happy.

"Can I tell him we talked?" she asked.

"Uh…I don't know." I wasn't sure how he would feel about it.

"I'd like to," she said. "If you'll allow me. I think he deserves to know that he has great friends who would do anything to see him happy. Besides, it'll be a lot easier for me to tell him the truth than make up a lie."

I definitely didn't want their relationship to start off in a shaky way. "Yeah, you can tell him."

"Okay, great. Well, it was nice to meet all of you. I'm really glad we talked. I've been doing a lot of thinking and this pointed me in the right direction. Nathan and I were having dinner together when we ran into my parents… They were pretty appalled by the idea of us getting back together. That was when I started to realize it would never work. They both love Ryker."

"He's easy to love," I said. "You really couldn't find a better guy."

She finally smiled, looking as beautiful as she did in the pictures Ryker showed me. "I know. I'm very lucky."

13

RYKER

I sat on my couch with my beer in my hand. There wasn't anything good on TV, so I put on a hockey game. I wasn't a big fan of the sport, but at least it was a sport. It was better than all the other crap that was on.

I texted Rae and asked if the gang wanted to hang out tonight before they flew out in the morning, but she never texted me back. Maybe she and Zeke wanted to have a romantic dinner at a fancy restaurant in the city. Maybe Rex and Kayden were doing the same thing. I understood and didn't take it personally.

My phone lit up with a text message from Austen. *Can I come by?*

I sat upright and put my beer on the coaster. Anytime Austen texted me, she had my full attention. I didn't care about food or alcohol anymore. *Sure.* She wasn't spending the evening with Nathan, which was a relief. I only had one more week of this misery before she picked me or Nathan.

She better pick me.

I'll be there in ten minutes.

I was already dressed and the housecleaners had just finished cleaning the place, so there was nothing for me to do. I looked at the clock and counted down the minutes until she arrived. Like a dog waiting for their owner, it felt like an eternity.

Longer than an eternity.

Finally, she knocked on the door.

I was nervous like usual. Anytime I was about to interact with her, I felt the adrenaline spike in my blood. Any moment with her could be my last. She could say those dreaded words any day now, that she would rather be with Nathan instead of me.

I wouldn't be a graceful loser. I'd tell her she was making a mistake and beg her to reconsider even though she'd already made up her mind. If it were any other woman, I'd pretend to be indifferent just to save my pride.

But I didn't play games with Austen.

I wore my heart on my sleeve.

I opened the door and saw her standing on the other side in a dark blue dress. It tied around her neck, making a deep V in the front. I could see the flawless skin of her chest and the slight swell of her breasts. As much as I wanted to stare, I remained a perfect gentleman and didn't look. "Hey, sweetheart." I ushered her inside then shut the door. "Wanna grab a beer?" There was nothing to watch here, and as much as I wouldn't mind making out on my bed, I didn't trust myself not to take it a step further. Three weeks without any action was getting to me.

"No. I just wanted to talk."

"Oh?" Fuck, it was happening. She was here to tell me she picked Nathan. That was why she was so quiet, so timid. She stopped by without giving me much of a head's up because she just left Nathan's.

Shit, this hurt.

It hurt more than I expected it to.

"I told Nathan it wasn't going to work out..." She looked at me with those pretty eyes, looking like a porcelain doll. Her lips were painted red with lipstick, and her mascara made her eyes stunning. Her words sounded too good to be true, like a mirage that I hadn't really witnessed.

"You're picking me?" I needed crystal clear confirmation. I needed to know this was real, not one of my dreams. This was the beginning of something new, something beautiful.

"Yeah."

All my limbs felt numb, just as they did after an intense exercise session. I was breathing normally, but for some reason, I wasn't getting enough air. I needed to breathe deeper, longer. My fingers flexed toward my palm, forming fists even though I wasn't angry.

Austen stared at me as she waited for a response. Her expression hadn't changed during the encounter. She was just as timid as before, borderline shy.

"You're sure?"

She nodded. "Yes."

The nightmare was finally over. I didn't have to think about what she was doing with him on their dates. I didn't have to ask Madeline how Austen felt about him. Now he was gone.

"I was trying to chase what Nathan and I used to have. I needed to realize that relationship was gone… that our love died a long time ago. But I've accepted that it is over, everything disappeared the day I caught him with Lily. I know he's sorry about what he did, but I could never trust him again. And why would I want to try when I have you?" She never looked more beautiful than she did now, looking up at me like I was the only thing that mattered. "You're everything I've ever wanted in a happily ever after. You're my best friend and the best sex I've ever had. I can tell you anything and everything. And when we're apart, I'm never worried about what you're doing. It's so easy to trust you, so easy to fall for you. I'm just sorry I made you wait this long. You didn't deserve that."

"You were worth the wait, sweetheart."

She tucked her hair behind her ear, a smile forming on her lips. "Rae talked to me this morning…"

What did she say? "Sorry?"

"Rae texted me from your phone last night. We got breakfast this morning. I was expecting you but got her and some of her friends instead."

The gang talked to Austen? Behind my back?

"She said you aren't in love with her anymore. She can tell. I'm all you ever talk about…and you really care about me. She told me I would be stupid to pick Nathan over you. She's right."

Rae did that for me? She flew all the way here just to fix my love life. It was incredible, but when I thought about the kind of person she was, it really wasn't that surprising. "I don't know what to say…"

"You don't have to say anything. I already had my doubts about Nathan. My parents adore you and despise him. Madeline made her feelings very clear…Jared isn't a fan of him either. I knew I was forcing it, trying to chase something that didn't exist anymore. And when Rae told me you didn't have feelings for her anymore, I knew I should choose you."

I wasn't sure why Rae said that. I never said anything of the sort. But when I considered it, I knew I didn't think about Rae the way I used to. Thoughts of her didn't keep me up in the middle of the night. I didn't wonder what her and Zeke were doing while I was home alone. All my thoughts were comprised of one person—Austen. "That woman is right about everything. So if that's what she says, it must be true."

She moved closer to me, only leaving a few inches between us. "So…"

"So…"

"You'll have me then?" Her hands rested against my stomach, her fingertips slightly digging into me.

"You already know the answer to that, sweetheart." My hand moved up her cheek and into her hair. My thumb brushed against her soft skin, and I remembered all the times I kissed her when she was just a friend, a hookup. Now she meant so much more to me. My heart had been broken, but without even realizing it, Austen put it back together.

Her hand wrapped around my wrist, and she looked up at me with that cute smile on her lips. "I thought I would always be scared to be with someone else…but you've made it so easy. I'm not afraid. I know you won't hurt me."

"Because we're best friends. Friends don't hurt each other."

"But they have great sex."

The corner of my mouth rose in a smile. "Exactly." I

wasn't afraid of getting hurt either, despite what happened with Rae. I should have fought for Austen sooner, but somehow I got her anyway. It worked out in the end, and I learned my lesson.

I pulled her into me and finally kissed her in a way I never have before. Now that this was real, we were in this together, everything felt different. Her lips were different, her breathing was different. It was more than a physical embrace, a charged touch. It felt like I'd been kissing her my whole life but I didn't recall those memories until now. It was so easy with Austen, even easier than it was with Rae.

I guided her into the bedroom, needing to be inside her sooner rather than later. I didn't want to jump into bed because I was horny. I just wanted to feel our bodies move together, our mouths cherish one another. I wanted my woman underneath me, taking every inch of me. It was just her and me and no one else, and I wanted to treasure every single moment of her. I needed to make up for the lost time, to erase every embrace Nathan ever gave her.

I needed to make her mine.

I walked into the kitchen and made a pot of coffee. Austen was still asleep, and after the rendezvous we had last night, she wouldn't be awake for a while. Rae slipped my mind the second Austen's mouth was on mine, so I hadn't thought about the incredible gesture she made for me. Now that I had the opportunity, I watched the coffee seep as I called her.

She answered after a few rings. "I'm surprised you're awake." Judging by her playfulness, Austen told her she was going to talk to me.

"Me too. But it's hard for me to sleep in."

"And it's also hard for you to get a job," she teased.

"It's not hard. I just don't want to."

Rae chuckled over the phone. "Is she there?"

"She's still asleep."

"Uh, she sleeps in like I do."

I watched the coffee drip into the pot, making ripples with every splash. Every time the water moved through the filter system, it made a loud gargling sound. The bedroom was on the other side of the apartment so it wouldn't wake up Austen. "She told me what you did."

Rae stayed quiet.

"Thank you." I should be mad she went through my phone like that, but since I got Austen in the end, I didn't care. "You always fix people...and I'm glad you fixed me."

"I didn't fix you, Ryker. I just gave Austen a little nudge..."

"No. You put up with my bullshit for a long time, and

you taught me what love really means. Without you, I never would have been prepared for Austen, to love her. I would have been the immature jerk that only cared about himself. I'll never be able to thank you enough for changing me into who I am now."

Rae didn't say anything for a long time. "I didn't change you, Ryker. You did that on your own."

"But you're the reason for it. It didn't work out between us, but it still worked out in the end. Austen is everything I could ever want in another person. I'm not gonna let her go. I'm not gonna fuck it up."

"I know you won't, Ryker."

"And it's all because of you."

"Well, she's pretty incredible. I really like her."

"She's cute, isn't she?" I asked with a smile. "She's got that cute little nose and those pretty eyes. And her body…" I whistled under my breath.

"Well, I didn't notice all of that," she said with a laugh. "But I liked her. I understand why you're so fond of her. Have you told her you love her yet?"

I crossed my arms over my chest at the question. I hadn't even truly admitted to myself how I felt. It'd been floating in the back of my mind for a long time, but I never had the balls to actually accept the truth. "No."

"Don't stall, alright? Because she loves you too."

My heart skipped a beat. "She said that?"

"No. I can just tell."

"How do you know everything?" Rae was the wisest person I'd ever met. She had to grow up when she was sixteen, so she became an adult long before her time. She was understanding and compassionate, and she knew how to stand up for herself too.

She shrugged. "I know I *don't* know everything. So I'm always learning."

In a strange way, that made sense. "Well, thank you. I don't know how to say it better than that."

"You don't need to. You would have done the same for me."

When she was with Zeke, I tried to steal her away. It wasn't my finest hour. But when Zeke broke her heart, I tried to get her back together with him because I knew it was the right thing to do. Perhaps I have grown. "When are you guys leaving?"

"At noon."

I eyed the time on the microwave. "You wanna get breakfast?"

"All of us?"

"Yeah." I grinned. "I'll bring my girlfriend."

"Good. We prefer her company over yours anyway."

"Are you a really good bowler?" Austen asked. "Since you own a bowling alley."

Rae rolled her eyes. "You'd think, right?"

Rex placed his hand over her face so we couldn't look at Rae anymore. "Not really. I won the lottery and tried to invest my money into something."

"So he bought a business he knows nothing about." Rae pushed his hand down. "So when the bowling alley nearly went under, Zeke and I had to put money into the place and revamp it. Thankfully, it's been a success ever since then."

"That was really nice of you guys," Austen said.

"We're family," Zeke said. "So we kinda had to do it."

"I never asked for anything," Rex said defensively. "I was prepared to lose everything rather than take your money."

"I know," Rae said. "But good thing we stepped in and saved the only wealth you had left. I had my own selfish interests tied up in the situation…so I was pretty determined to make it work."

"What interests?" Austen asked.

"He was living with me at the time," Rae said. "And he was a goddamn nightmare. He was driving me up the wall with all his dirty clothes on the floor, his dishes in the sink, and always having porn on in the living room."

Austen laughed. "Wow. In the living room?"

"I wasn't doing anything," Rex explained. "I just had it on. You know, background noise. Like when you leave

Friends on in the background while you're reading a book or something."

"Porn and *Friends* are not the same thing," Rae said. "Just admit it. You were a total pig."

Rex shrugged in guilt.

"Anyway," Rae said. "To answer your question, he doesn't know the first thing about bowling."

I rested my arm over the back of the booth with Austen pressed into my side. She got along with everyone as well as I hoped she would. Austen had a great sense of humor, and she was much smarter than I was. She and Rae were a lot alike.

"So, you're a brainiac or something?" Rex asked.

I kicked him under the table.

"Ouch." He leaned forward and breathed through the pain. "What? That's what you said."

Austen looked at me, a smile on her face. "A brainiac, huh?"

"A hot brainiac," I said. "I told them you graduated from MIT."

"Whoa," Zeke said. "That's seriously impressive. Very cool."

"Thanks." Austen looked down when too much attention was on her. "I'm in charge of the marketing department at work. I like it."

"Maybe I should have gone to college," Rex said.

"No." Kayden rubbed his chest. "You turned out great, Rex. You don't need to change a thing."

He grinned and wrapped his arm around her shoulders. "I love this woman right here."

"She's pretty great for you," Rae said. "So don't blow it."

"Never." He rubbed his nose against Kayden's before he kissed her.

Austen smiled at their affection. "It'll be weird telling my parents my boyfriend is unemployed…"

"I'm not unemployed," I corrected.

"You don't have a job, right?" Austen asked. "That's the definition."

"But I'm not broke and lazy," I argued.

"You're definitely lazy," she said with a laugh.

"I'm basically a financial advisor for myself," I said. "Big difference. And I hit the gym every day. You think I'd look this sexy if I just sat around playing video games all day?"

Austen shrugged.

"So make sure you give your parents all the facts." I didn't want them to get the wrong impression of what kind of guy I was.

Rae looked at her watch. "Well, we should get going otherwise we'll miss our flight. It was nice getting breakfast with you guys before we took off."

"Always a pleasure," I said. "We'll stop by when we come to Seattle to visit my family."

"Perfect." Rae scooted out of the booth along with the others. "Until next time." She rose on her tiptoes and hugged me.

I returned the embrace and felt the absence of anything romantic in my chest. I hugged her just as I would hug Kayden. There was nothing there but great fondness. I hugged her back and felt the comfort of our friendship, our bond. "Keep COLLECT going, alright?"

"Like I have any influence on that place."

"Yes, you do. You're the best employee there." I let her go then patted her on the back. "Without scientists doing all the work, we wouldn't be able to do our jobs."

"You make me sound more important than I really am, but thank you." She turned to Austen next then hugged her. "It was so nice to meet you. You can give me a call if he starts to drive you crazy."

Austen hugged her back then laughed. "I'll keep that in mind."

We said goodbye to everyone else, and to my surprise, Zeke hugged me. "Take care, man. If things don't work out here, you always have a home in Seattle —and not just at Mega Shake."

Everything he said meant the world to me. I used to be close with Zeke and Rex until I hurt Rae. They turned their backs on me quicker than I turned my back on Rae. Having their friendship again felt nice. I didn't realize how much I missed it until then. "Thanks, man. It means a lot."

"I'll call you if Rae starts to get on my nerves," he said with a smile.

"Yeah, whatever," Rex said. "You know I'm the first person on your speed dial."

"Who uses speed dial anymore?" Kayden said. "Isn't everything on phones speed dial?"

After a wave, they all left and got into the cab. They needed to swing by their hotel and pick up their luggage before they headed to the airport.

I watched them go, feeling a little sad that they were gone. I had my own friends in the city, but that group of people filled a different kind of void in my chest. Even when I was alone, I never really felt alone because I knew they were out there.

Austen circled her arm around my waist. "I really like your friends."

"Yeah? Even Rex?"

"They're good people. Especially Rex. He's funny."

I circled my arm around her waist and walked outside with her. The momentary sadness I felt was quickly gone when I remembered the woman beside me. She was everything I ever needed. "There's something I've been meaning to tell you."

"What's up?" she asked.

"Rae told me to tell you that I loved you. She said you felt the same way."

Surprise burned in her eyes at the nonchalant way I blurted that out.

"So before I say it...you feel the same way, right?"

She moved closer into my chest then interlocked our fingers together. Over a foot shorter than me but taller in presence, this woman was incredible. She had a wild unpredictability and fierce sense of loyalty. "That woman is always right."

I got the answer I wanted. "I love you, Austen. And I want to love you for the rest of my life." I already lost one incredible woman, and there was no way I was gonna lose an even better one. Austen completed me in a way Rae never did. It made me wonder if Rae and I didn't work out because we were destined for other people. I didn't believe in that soul mate bullshit, but I definitely believed in what was right in front of me.

With this woman, I would always wear my heart on my sleeve. I would take advantage of every single day just to tell her I loved her. My life's purpose would be to make her smile, to make her feel safe with me. She no longer wore Nathan's scars because I'd kissed them away. I'd give her everything she needed, and she would give me everything I'd been living without.

Tears welled in her eyes when she heard me say it for the first time. I'd never seen Austen cry before, not like this. Seeing the moisture pool in her eyes while she smiled at the same time was a gorgeous sight. "I love you too…"

My entire body burned white-hot and cold at the same time. Hearing those words didn't make me scared. They only made me excited for everything up ahead. "You wanna go out for a romantic meal to celebrate? Or skip to the good stuff back at my place?"

She circled her arms around my neck and pressed her forehead to mine. "Let's go to your place, get naked, and then order a pizza."

That was the best plan I'd ever heard. "I think I love you even more now."

EPILOGUE

R YKER

"Are you nervous?" Rex leaned against the doorframe in his suit and watched me look at myself in the mirror. "Because you look nervous."

I adjusted my tie for the twelfth time. "I'm not nervous."

"Leave the guy alone." Zeke sat in the chair against the desk and checked his watch. "Every guy gets nervous on his wedding day."

"I'm not nervous," I repeated.

"You look nervous." Rex looked at my face in the reflection of the mirror. "You got some sweat on your forehead, you can't tie a tie... You're in bad shape."

Zeke glared at him. "Would you just shut up?"

"I'm not judging," Rex said quickly. "If I were getting

married, I'd be a total wreck too."

I turned around, giving up on the tie. "I'm not a wreck. I'm not nervous. I'm more excited to get married than she is. I can guarantee that."

Rex grinned from ear-to-ear. "Aww, that's sweet."

Zeke dragged his flattened hand across his neck. "Just leave the guy alone."

"I wonder what she looks like." I stood with my hands in my pockets, imaging how pretty my future wife would look in her wedding dress.

Rex shrugged. "I can go check if you want."

"No, you're staying right here," I said quickly. My brother just went to get me a coffee to keep me awake. We were out late last night hitting the bars in Seattle. In hindsight, it was a stupid decision to make.

The door opened, and Rae walked inside, fitted in her pink bridesmaid dress. "Ryker, can I talk to you for a minute?" For a happy occasion such as this, she seemed awfully serious. She kept the door open and nodded for the guys to walk out.

"Is everything okay?" I asked.

"Yeah, it's fine." She was such a bad liar. "Rex, Zeke, go."

Rex straightened and dropped his arms to his sides. "Maybe we can help—"

"Go. Now." She walked farther inside and pointed to the hallway.

Zeke knew she meant business, so he walked into the hallway. Rex followed a moment later.

Rae shut the door then walked up to me, looking even more nervous now that Rex and Zeke weren't there.

Now I was terrified. "What is it, Rae?"

"It's Austen...she's getting cold feet."

Fuck no. "What does that mean?"

"She's just panicking because she's scared right now."

"Scared of what?" I demanded. "We're perfect for each other. We're made for each other. What's there to be afraid of?" I couldn't keep my voice down because my anger was officially in charge. I wasn't letting her walk out on me, not when it was a mistake.

"I think it's because of Nathan. I think all of this is making her think about that day when she bought her wedding dress..."

The second she said the words, I realized how insensitive I'd been. The thought didn't even cross my mind. I proposed to her, planned the wedding with her, and had a great time at the rehearsal dinner. I didn't even think of the fact she'd done most of this already— with someone who broke her heart. "Shit..."

"I know she loves you. You just need to talk to her."

"I'm not supposed to see her."

"Then close your eyes. She just needs some comfort right now."

I'd been nothing but faithful to her. I hadn't even looked at another woman. But I didn't let myself get offended by Austen's insecurity. I understood where all of this was coming from. I promised to love her no matter what, and I would talk her off the ledge. "Okay."

"Come on." Rae led me down the hall in the hotel until we reached the bridal suite. She walked inside first.

I stood at the door and waited.

"I need you to stand behind this divider," Rae said.

"Why?" Austen spoke with a weak voice, sounding nothing like herself.

"Ryker is coming in here to talk to you. I don't want him to see you."

"You told him?" she snapped. "I didn't want him to know I was feeling this way. I wasn't going to walk out on him—"

"He knows that. He understands, Austen. He just wants to talk to you. Calm down, okay?"

"This isn't how I want to remember this day…"

"Trust me, when you're done talking to him, it's going to be perfect. I promise. Now please stand behind the divider."

Austen must have done it because she didn't say anything else.

Rae came back to the door. "You're on." She walked down the hallway and back into my suite where I'd been getting ready.

I took a deep breath before I walked inside. The bridal suite was three times as big as mine, with brushes, combs, and large bottles of hairspray everywhere. I could smell the perfume in the air and see the pairs of shoes off to the side.

I walked inside and approached the tall white divider that had been erected so the girls could get ready in private. The light from the window hit the divider perfectly so I could see her silhouette. The dress was skintight against her waist and flared out a little around her hips. Her hair was long and in curls. A flower crown rested on her head. I could see the shadow of the petals.

I placed my hand against the material even though I couldn't touch her. "Sweetheart, it's me."

She breathed deeply in response.

I listened to her shallow breaths and counted them.

"I want to marry you, Ryker. I don't know what Rae said, but that's never changed."

"I know, sweetheart. And I also know what it's like to be scared. I know what it's like to have all these incredible feelings that force you to shut down." Rae said three little words to me, and I ran quicker than an Olympic athlete. "I understand that you're nervous. It's perfectly normal."

"Are you nervous?"

I returned my hand to my pocket and considered my response. "No, not at all."

She sighed in disappointment.

"I'm not nervous because I know we're supposed to be together. I know you're the woman that I'm supposed to take care of. And I know I'm the only man you ever want to be with. Your doubts, your fears…they don't mean anything to me. They're temporary. They'll fade, Austen."

She sniffed behind the divider. "I guess…I'm scared because I love you so much. What we have is so incredible, and if I ever lost you—"

"Not gonna happen."

"I know. I just…"

"I'll never do what he did to you. I will always be right by your side, sweetheart."

"Even if we fight?" she whispered.

"Even if we fight."

"Even if things get rough?"

"No matter how rough it gets, I'll always be your husband. We'll always find our way back to each other. We're going to be together for the rest of our lives, sweetheart. Every single day. Nothing will ever come between us."

"How do you know that?"

All I had to do was look into that beautiful face and it would give me all the reassurance I needed. She was my best friend in the entire world. We were always honest with each other. Lies, infidelity, betrayal…none of those things would ever cross my mind. "Because we're meant for each other." I moved my around the divider so she could take it.

She stared at it for a moment before her small hand grabbed mine. Her engagement ring was cold against my fingers. She gripped me tightly, like this affection was exactly what she needed. She needed to feel me to know everything would be okay.

"I love you, Austen. I'm going to love you for the rest of my life."

She squeezed my hand. "I love you too, Ryker. I'm sorry I—"

"Don't apologize. This is how it's going to be every single day. When you fall, I'll pick you up. And when I fall, you'll be there for me."

She brought my hand to her lips and kissed it. "I'm so lucky to have you."

I was the lucky one—by a long shot. "You ready to get married?"

"Yes." Her breath fell across my knuckles. "More than anything."

"Are you ready for the honeymoon?" I asked with a smile in my voice.

She chuckled. "I think I'm more excited for that than the wedding."

"Bora Bora will be nice. It'll just be you and me in the middle of nowhere—making love."

"As husband and wife."

"Exactly." I gently pulled my hand away until it was on the other side of the divider.

"Does anyone else know about this?"

"Just you, me, and Rae."

"Okay. I wouldn't want your mother to start hating me."

"She loves you, sweetheart. You know that."

Austen sat in a chair behind the divider and crossed her legs.

I did what I set out to do. I calmed her down and made her remember why we were there. I reminded her that this was different than her first attempt, that we truly loved each other and were perfect for one another. "I'll see you at the end of the aisle."

"Actually, can you sit here with me for a while? We don't have to talk. I just want to be with you...keeps me calm."

I grabbed a chair and sat next to the divider and crossed my legs. "Anything for you, sweetheart." I stared at her silhouette and watched her breathe deeply. Slowly, her chest began to calm. Her breathing returned to normal, and we enjoyed each other's company.

She spoke so quietly I could barely hear her words. "I can't wait to marry you..."

"And I can't wait to marry you, Stone Cold."

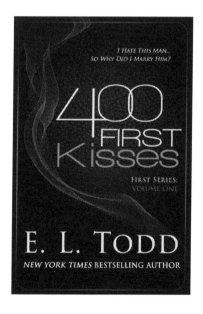

► FOL ◄

SEP 1 7 2024

Made in the USA
Columbia, SC
25 July 2017